AMAZON EXPEDIENT

PIERS ANTHONY

&

KENNETH KELLY

Other Books in This Series

Virtue Inverted
Amazon Expedient
Magenta Salvation
(Forthcoming)

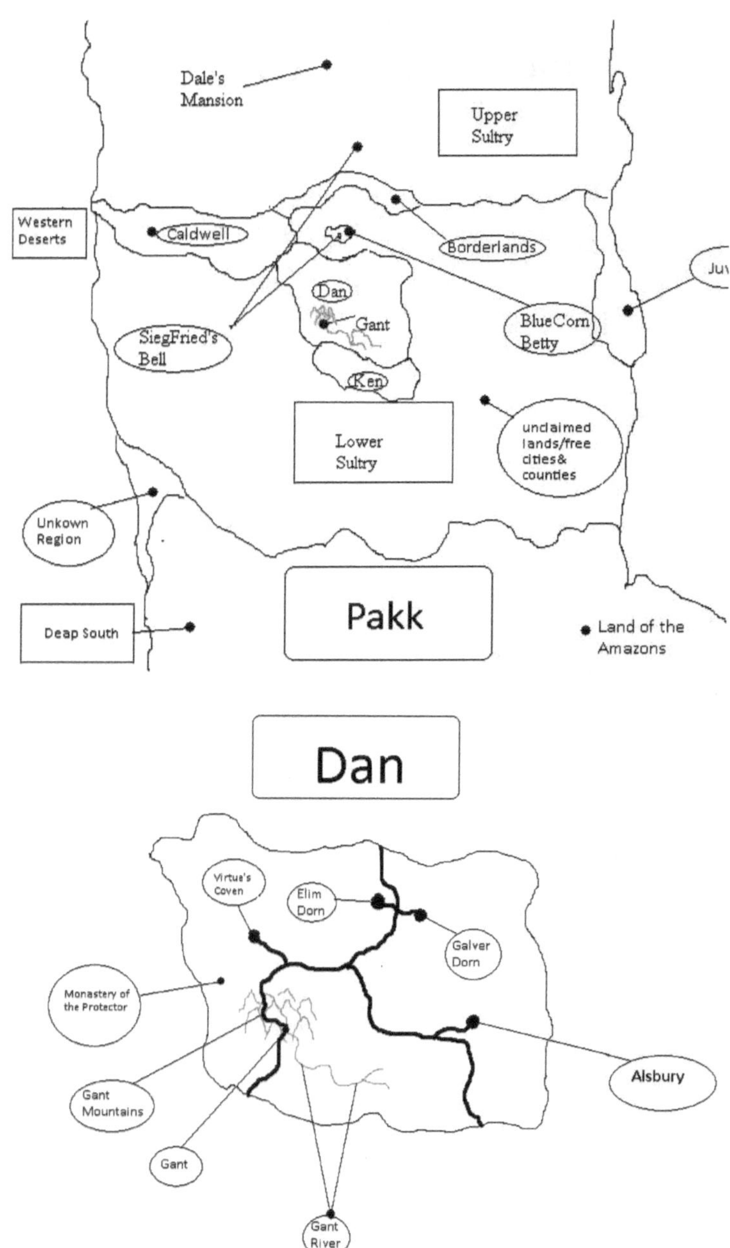

Dale's Mansion
Upper Sultry
Western Deserts
Caldwell
Borderlands
Juv
Dan
Gant
SiegFried's Bell
BlueCorn Betty
Ken
Lower Sultry
unclaimed lands/free cities & counties
Unkown Region
Deap South
Pakk
Land of the Amazons
Dan
Virtue's Coven
Elim Dorn
Galver Dorn
Monastery of the Protector
Alsbury
Gant Mountains
Gant
Gant River

Prologue

Toadstool Tortoise was, as his name implies, a large walking, talking tortoise. In other worlds, a walking, talking animal would be very out of place, but in Gold Mulch Wood, this sort of thing is quite normal. The Pawben met Toadstool when he first came to the Wood and the two quickly struck up a friendship. The little Beranger boy was just a baby at the time, and the Pawben was in a strange new world; naturally, he was quite startled to come across a creature such as the tortoise. It seemed to Pawben that the world he had come to, of which Gold Mulch Wood was but a small part, was a land of dreams and fairy tales. Things deemed impossible in many of the worlds he had previously visited had been spit out and collected here. He'd come to this world in order to save Dale Beranger's grandson from the horrors of his forefathers' homeland, in order to raise him in a peaceful, loving environment away from the likes of mercenaries, fallen inter-dimensional angels, vampires, werewolves, assassins, Sky Titans, and countless other beings that had made Pawben's life so hard. To be honest, Pawben stumbled across his current homestead quite on accident, as his self-named "world jumping," had gotten rusty in his advanced years. He wanted to take the boy back to Lower Sultry, Dan, and the land of his ancestors, but this present Wood was so peaceful that he doubted he'd live up to his intentions. Now, he trotted with long beard, bent back and bowed legs as the blond boy in the red felt cap ran circles around him with the little-big rat, Flack, clinging to his shoulder.

"Run faster, Pawben!" the boy yelled.

"I gladly will, if you'd care to trade bodies with me."

They eventually came to a little trail leading into the trees which led to a little house shaped like a huge white and red mushroom. Pawben saw the little welcome sign hanging on the little crooked door in the fat white stalk of the building, and was relieved that he'd be able to rest his feet. The door opened and Toadstool, wearing an apron and chef's hat, peeked his head out.

"Lateness is rudeness!" he shouted.

"What's the rush? Got a hot date?" Pawben responded.

The boy ran around Pawben and hugged Toadstool tightly, his little hands groping around the back of the tortoise's shell. The rat, glad to flee the boy's shoulder, ran up Toadstool's arm and across his shell. The tortoise yelled and danced a jig trying to get the rat off him.

"Get this vermin off me!" he screamed.

"You're asking this rude old man for help? That's wishful thinking," Pawben said, walking around them into the house. The rat jumped off and followed him over the threshold.

"Where's dinner?" the old man asked. Toadstool came into the living room, following the boy, and pointed at the rat.

"I'm half tempted to cook him!"

"Ol' Flack's harmless, but I won't be if you don't stick a plate of edibles in front of me. You know how I turn into the wicked witch of the west when I don't eat." Pawben said, tapping his staff on the wooden floor.

"Ok, grandma! Don't get your knickers in a twist."

Pawben giggled under his breath. They liked giving each other a hard time. He glanced around the room at the familiar sights. Toadstool was almost 5 feet tall, so the house was furnished to fit the average human. The bottom floor, which was the stalk, was living room, kitchen and dining room. A small staircase wound itself up into the cap of the mushroom, which doubled as a bedroom and private library. At the little table in the middle of the room, Toadstool had three plates, cutlery, and cups set out for his guests. Pawben and the boy sat down as Toadstool brought around a plate of cucumber sandwiches. The boy frowned and crossed his arms.

"I no like cucumber sandwiches!" he pouted.

"I know, which is why I made you this." Toadstool turned back to the kitchen counter and brought around a loaf of banana nut bread. The boy smiled from ear to ear and rubbed his hands together. He didn't even wait for the tortoise to pour them all a round of cider before tearing into the delicious treat. Pawben took a petite little sandwich wedge and took a bite. The cucumber was sliced extra thin the way he liked it, and he closed his eyes as he savored the wine-soaked cheese both he and the tortoise were so fond of. He washed it down with some cider and burped.

"Taste it twice!" The tortoise laughed.

Pawben noticed Flack looking at him from the floor by his feet, and despite that he'd warned the boy about feeding the animal table scraps in Toadstool's presence, he ripped off a piece of bread from his sandwich and tossed it to the rodent.

"Come on, man!" The tortoise rushed to grab the scrap but the rat was too quick, "If I let one animal eat from the table, pretty soon all kinds of animals will be begging me for food."

"You *ARE* an animal eating from the table, turtle boy, or did you forget?" Pawben smiled.

"I'm a tortoise, thank you very much." The turtle sat back down.

They continued munching while Toadstool complained about Flack. After catching the rat trying to crawl underneath his couch, Pawben made a comment without thinking.

"You know, that rat's almost as much of a nuisance as the real Flack was," Pawben said.

"No I don't know…You've mentioned this mysterious Flack about a hundred times since I met you, and you've never told me a word about him." Toadstool wiped his green mouth and leaned back in his chair, which had a concave backing to accommodate his shell.

"Yeah, Pawben, tell story!" the boy shouted, bouncing eagerly in his chair and breadcrumbs falling from his mouth.

"I don't know if you're old enough, yet. It's not a nice story to tell," Pawben said. He took another bite of his sandwich and prayed the conversation would move in a different direction. He had already decided that if he did tell the tale, it would be in his usual style, from third person perspective. It was for the boy's benefit, rather than Toadstool's, who already knew Pawben's true identity. He would reveal the truth about both himself and the boy's grandfather, Dale Beranger, once the lad was older.

"Oh, pollywog! When I was his age, I was already

hunting with my pa." Toadstool said, "Tell us the story, the lad can handle it."

"I guess you two aren't gonna leave me alone until I do. Well, it's a long, complicated tale. Get comfortable." Pawben motioned for the trio to move from the dining table to the couch, "I've told you both, to an extent, about how Benny Clout met Dale Beranger, Cycleze and Virtue, and how Benny and the latter helped Dale overcome his inner demons and follow a life of good deeds and service to others. Five years had passed relatively uneventfully since Benny had watched Dale and Nadia leave Gant to begin their lives together, not long after which he and Virtue got married."

"Wait, Pawben…I thought you were gonna tell us about the real Flack!" The boy looked quizzically at the old man.

"Flack is an integral part of this story, but he's far from the only important character. During the course of this tale, you will hear of other people, both men and women, human and non-human, good and evil; they have all affected my… err…Benny's life significantly."

The boy grabbed the rat and placed him in his lap, looking up at his guardian with the same awestruck face he always had when listening to one of Pawben's stories.

"But yes, boy, I'll tell you about Flack."

CHAPTER 1

Maniacal laughter sounded as the green orb filled Benny's vision. It seemed as if he was frozen in stasis, unable to move his body or avert his gaze from the symbol of evil that burned into his head. Tentacles of ice wrapped around his arms, legs, chest and throat, choking the life out him. Still the laughter continued. The green orb became clear and Benny realized that it was a single, giant eye, the pupil throbbing and pulsating with the eerie light. He was in agony, but he couldn't scream or even whimper. A voice like raging thunder filled his ears, and Benny's fear was made complete.

"You'll never stop us," it said, "we're coming!"

"No!" Benny screamed.

He nearly jumped out of his skin as he erupted from the covers of his bed. The scar on both sides of his mouth was aching severely and he was drenched in cold sweat, breathing as if he'd just run 14 miles through the steepest passes of the Gant Mountains. It was dark at first, and he feared that he had awoken from one nightmare only to appear in another, but soon his eyes adjusted and he saw that he was in his own familiar room at the Fox Den. Falling back onto his pillow, the young man realized the body which so often slept next to his was now absent. It was still night, as Benny deducted by two mirrored crescent moons, one blue and the other green as they shone their light through the window on the other side of the room. Benny looked around, and was relieved to see his wife sitting at a table in the far corner of the room, her face buried in a thick book about telepathy, squinting in the dim candlelight. She saw his frightened look and left her studies to sit beside him on the bed. She held his sweaty head gently against her bosom, his sweat being absorbed by her nightgown.

"It's the same dream, Virtue," he said.

"It's only a dream, love," she said, stroking his hair, "They don't mean anything."

Benny knew Virtue was only saying this to comfort him. Dreams were not something to be taken for granted, as Virtue had often told Benny in the past. As an extra means of income, she often interpreted dreams and visions, not excluding those of herself and Benny, to make predictions about the future. Nothing serious was ever exposed, but Benny's recurring dreams had been the first Virtue had ever failed to decipher using her newly developed skills of telepathy. Benny could not use these same means of extrasensory perception that Virtue had recently learned, but he knew when she was being insincere.

"You know that's not true, Virtue. It's the exact same terrible vision, over and over again-- the same green eye… the same voice…the tentacles, choking me…"

"Just because I can't decode your subconscious doesn't mean they're anything to worry about. My studies have even told me that not all dreams transmit foresights or prophecies, and you do drink a lot of that *special* cider with

Jack at dinner." She smiled at the last comment. Benny was not an alcoholic, but he was fond of Jack's spiked cider, which had been known to cause hallucinations.

"Maybe so…still, I worry," he said.

"Then let me do the worrying," she replied. She leaned over Benny and passionately pressed her warm lips against his. After being married for almost 5 years, her kisses still made Benny weak at the knees, even though he was lying down. She continued to rock him as a cool breeze wafted in from the nighttime mountain air. The pain of Benny's scar began to dissipate and he closed his eyes. The dream didn't come back.

Chapter 2

During the years since he'd last seen Dale and Nadia, Benny had grown significantly in stature. From the scrawny, effeminate 5'7" he'd been when he'd first fought Dale, Benny had sprouted to a muscular 6'1". He'd let his hair grow somewhat since he'd shaved his head at the request of the dying Cycleze, but not nearly as long as it had been, and its silvery-blond hue had darkened to a sandy brown. He kept it slicked back and tucked behind his ears, and because of the pain it caused him to shave, he usually sported a scraggly beard except for very special occasions. The pain was largely due to an attempt to have the scar repaired about a year after Dale left, and the traveling surgeon Benny had hired had reduced the size of his mouth to what it had been, but had somehow unnaturally folded the skin when sewing it up. Ever since then, his mouth was easily irritated. He couldn't even sleep on his side anymore because of the pressure the pillow would place against the scar, inflaming it. Everyone had warned him to leave it alone, but in his vanity he'd hoped he could somewhat regain his former looks. This didn't stop Benny from continuing his life, though.

Benny realized after his two duals with Dale that he

lacked proper skills in sword fighting. Therefore, he enlisted Laughing Jack Baldwin, his friend and proprietor of the Fox Den Inn and Tavern, to train with him. Jack had been a magnificent swordsman in his younger days, even boasting that he had once bested Dale in a friendly dual. However, years of inactivity at the inn and a bad knee had greatly reduced his skills. Still, he was more than enough for Benny to handle, who longed for the day he could best Jack in a fight. It took several years, but that day finally came.

"I've gotcha now, boy!" Jack screamed.

"Dream on, grandpa!" Benny retorted.

Jack came at Benny with a long, arching swipe which Benny met with his own wooden training sword, sidestepping as Jack stumbled past. Benny countered off the block with a strike aimed at Jack's neck, but the old man had some agility left after all, and raised a block just in time. They continued locking swords in the clearing behind the river, behind the main building of the Inn. Kids sometimes came to watch their training, but not on this day, which allowed the two to step things up a notch.

"Not bad, kid," Jack said, faking a blow to Benny's head and redirecting it at his knees, "Just be grateful I got this bum leg."

"Or that sack of flour around your waist!" Benny yelled. He locked swords and came in close to Jack before pushing off and throwing a spinning back-foot kick some foreigner had taught him a week before. It caught Jack square in the solar plexus, but the old man had trained himself to expel the air from his lungs before such a blow. It still stung though, and while he did his best to reduce his injury, Benny's kick caused him to pause for a split second.

"Aha!" Benny shouted.

As strong as Benny had gotten, Jack's age and experience had ingrained a natural stamina Benny didn't yet have. This particular match had been going on for almost 20 minutes so far, one of their longest bouts, and Benny's arms and legs were tired. Jack had landed a few solid punches and elbows of his own. However, unbeknownst to him, Jack was thinking the exact opposite: that it was he that was near the point of exhaustion. Then, Jack went all out. He slashed at Benny from every direction; vertical, horizontal, slashing, stabbing, and throwing as many kicks with his good leg as he could muster. Benny was completely flustered. The times Jack had unleashed flurries like this before, Benny would always give up or "die." He knew Jack couldn't last long in this state, and hoped he could ride it out. Finally, Jack seemed to stop in mid-strike. He was breathing heavier than Benny had ever heard him, and in the split second it took him to react, Benny knocked Jack's sword out of the way and then moved low, pulling Jacks bad leg out from under him with what would be the flat edge of the blade. It connected right at his ankle, and in a split second Jack was on his back with the point of the wooden sword at his neck.

"Want any more?" Jack said between short, strong breaths.

"No...I give up." Benny responded.

He stuck the wooden sword back in his belt and lifted Jack to his feet. After a few seconds of leaning on his friend, Jack caught his breath and started laughing. Benny rolled his eyes and walked his mentor back to the dining hall. Benny had finally bested his friend, but rather than be elated, he was sad that Jack had aged so much in the last five years. When they first started training, Jack seemed invincible. Soon, Benny doubted Jack would be able to keep up with him. They walked into the dining hall and sat down at a nearby table.

"My stomach's in my throat," Jack inhaled sharply. "Since when did you learn to kick like that?"

"That foreigner, Kang. He taught me a few other tricks, too. I could show you if you want?" Benny smirked.

"No, I think my fighting days are just about over. I thought me sparring with you would get me back into shape, but I think my body's beginning to fall apart." Benny's heart sank. Jack really was getting old.

"You're trying to do too much, Jack. You're running this place and training with me at the same time. Let me take over some of the chores." Benny suggested.

"No, no, no. You and Virtue already do enough. That little 'dream reading' thing she does brings in quite a bit of extra coin, and you bring shipments from Down Mountain."

"That's only once a month, though. Let me take care of some things. I'll hire a carpenter to replace the bridge, get some artists to touch up the frescoes here in the dining hall, and anything else that needs doing. You can just relax and greet guests at night and stuff like that."

"Well, I guess I wouldn't mind having some extra time on my hands. I could spend some more time with that older widow who just moved in," Jack's eye lit up at that last statement, "Yeah…sure, Benny. Take the reins for a while. We'll see how it goes." Jack smiled and walked back to the kitchen to prepare things for that night.

A few years prior, Jack broke down and finally hired Nap, the annoying Halfling, to work at the Fox Den. At times it seemed more trouble than it was worth, but once Benny took over more and more of the tasks of running the establishment, he was grateful for what little Nap did.

During the days Benny prepared meals for the evening's guests, oversaw the bridge replacement and fresco touch-ups, and sent Nap once a month to get food, barrels of beer and mead, and other necessities. At night he was able to relax a little, letting Virtue give her psychic readings and dream interpretation. It brought in quite a bit of coin, as most of the farmers, peasants, and even the dwarfs who worked in the local mines would come, hoping to hear of good fortune in their futures and to better understand their dreams. Jack regained some of his liveliness, frequently visiting a widowed woman who had moved into Benny's old hovel in town (with Jack asking for an occasional bite from Virtue to aid him in his romantic affairs). Benny quickly realized why Jack had been lagging in their fighting, as the duties of running an inn and tavern were no easy job. Several weeks passed by, and nothing eventful happened. Benny began secretly hoping some excitement would come along and swoop him up in a grand adventure. He should've been careful about what he wished for, because that's exactly what happened.

CHAPTER 3

It was a typical, lively night, and Benny and Virtue had just finished a song and dance number. They never liked to let one dance simmer for too long, and so decided to entertain the crowds by doing a little role reversal, Benny wearing a crudely made dress and mop-wig, while Virtue dressed as knight, saving Benny, who was the designated damsel in distress. The patrons got a hoot out of it, including a couple of surly dwarves from the mines, who kept cat calling Benny and throwing coins to him. It was after they'd finished, Virtue cradling Benny in her arms when he heard a loud voice directed at him.

"Wow, Ben. I don't think you'll have much luck passing off as a gal if you plan on dressing like that full-time. You ain't as pretty as you used to be!" the man said. The accent sounded familiar, but Benny couldn't place it.

He looked up at the figure who'd just come out of the pouring rain. He was a tall, handsome man with a big nose and neatly groomed blond hair. He wore a brown travelers' cloak over chain mail, and a hefty sword slung across his back. He had a kind smile, but Benny sensed a playfulness that could get carried away. *Who's this joker? I know I've seen that face before,* Benny thought.

"Oh, come on Benny. Don't act like you don't know me," the man turned to a companion who was walking in behind him, "Benny, here, is acting like he don't know me from turd pie."

Benny almost fainted when he saw the man's companion, but held himself together. It was an orc with blueish-green skin and wiry hair. He had fangs jutting out of both top and bottom lip, and he had ornamental barbs that looked like porcupine needles embedded into his head. He had very ugly features, and walked with the awkward bow-legged swagger Benny had seen in orcs passing. Benny knew not to judge a book by its cover, since he himself wasn't the prettiest thing to look at, so he politely smiled at both and went to greet them.

"I'm sorry, gents, but I don't think I've seen you two around here before," Benny replied, grasping both the man and the orc's hand, crossed over each other, at once.

"Oh, now you're being silly, Ben." The man winked and led his companion to the table underneath the rainbow gnome fresco.

"It's probably the nose job," the orc said in a squeaky voice, pointing at the man's face.

"Oh, I'd forgotten. Now look who's acting foolish." Benny noted a sudden change from the country-boy accent the man had when he entered to a very familiar, well-spoken tone.

The man reached up to his hairline and began to pull the skin right off his face. Benny gasped until he realized that it wasn't actually skin, but some type of prosthetic face covering, so well blended in with the rest of the man's face he didn't even notice. As the man peeled the mask off his forehead, the nose went along with it, revealing a hideous scar and two gaping nostril holes. The man then pulled off the apparently fake goatee that had surrounded his lips, showing off the huge hole in his upper lip. Benny let out a loud chuckle when he realized it was Dale Beranger.

"Dale!" Benny pulled him out of his chair and grasped him in a bear hug that shocked the man.

"Careful, boy. You're a lot stronger than you used to be." They both laughed.

"Hey, fella," Virtue said, walking over and kissing him on the cheek. He gave a respectful bow and kissed her hand.

"How do you fare, my lady?" Virtue blushed and looked at Benny, who couldn't offer much help because of how much he was laughing.

"Oh, knock it off, Dale. You're no gentleman," she said.

"I am now, thanks to you." Dale turned and pointed at his companion, "I wish I could say the same for this sot."

The orc smiled, revealing the full length of his tusks. Then the orc started laughing too, a high pitched wine that almost hurt Benny's ears.

"Are you going to introduce us, Dale?" Virtue asked.

"Oh, yes. Forgive me. This is Uubum Ma Gug." Dale sat and patted the orc on the shoulder.

"You can call me Bum, for short," the orc said.

"How did you two meet?" Benny asked.

Dale and Bum looked at each other with somber, respected looks. Then Bum spoke. "I'm the orc who killed Dale's brother."

"Sit down and we'll explain," Dale said.

The story Dale and Bum told Virtue and Benny was a true testament to the power of love and forgiveness over hatred and revenge. Dale's brother, whose name was Zorn, had gone hunting for some wild deer one day, and unbeknownst to him, Bum had been hunting in the same area. Bum had seen Zorn moving through some bushes and mistook him for wild game, shooting him with his crossbow. When he found Zorn dying, Bum took him to Alsbury for immediate care, but being pierced through a lung, Zorn soon died. Bum was ashamed, and exiled himself from his tribe before Dale killed the orphans and led the revolt against Bum's tribe. When he found out what had happened, he fell into despair and became a mercenary, very similar to Dale. Then, about three years ago, Dale and Nadia came across Bum in a bazaar in Narbonia, a town in the country of Juvia, east of Dan and located on the coast. Dale apologized to Bum, explained how he'd been tricked and manipulated by Cycleze and how Virtue and Benny had helped free him from his evilness. Bum was so moved that he renounced his mercenary ways, and on that same day helped Dale defeat an invasion of pirates from the countries across the Great Ocean. They vowed to be eternally indebted to each other, and considered themselves brothers.

"And here we are," Bum said. He ladled chicken soup into his mouth, which had been brought by a timid Nap.

"So now we're taking some time off to come back here and help Jack for a while." Dale said, "Bum and I have been doing a lot of work in Juvia helping the merchant guilds, investigating and dismantling a gang of thieves and whatnot. Stuff like that."

"That's very commendable, Beranger." Nap said. Dale frowned and looked at the Halfling, who whimpered at the man's glare.

"Call me Dale. Just Dale. Beranger is dead."

Benny was very moved by the way Dale had completely changed his ways. When he'd last seen Dale, the man was confused by his newfound conscience. Before his conversion bite, Beranger was a proud, bigoted sociopath who killed for revenge, personal gain, and for fun. He was a domineering bully who treated people like dirt. This man was completely different. While Dale still had a touch of sarcasm about him, Benny could sense an inner kindness that had been absent before. Benny looked down at the fake face prosthetic, which Dale had rolled up and laid beside his mug of cider.

"Nice, isn't it?" Dale asked, "A wizard made it for me. He enchanted it so that when I put it on, it blends in with my face completely. It even feels real. I love it, but Nadia doesn't seem to like it much."

"Speaking of Nadia, where is she?" Virtue asked. Benny hadn't even thought about Nadia since Dale came into the Fox Den, but now he was a bit curious. Still, he was worried that Virtue's imploring attitude would start trouble.

"Oh, her? She's just visiting some long lost family a little north of here."

"Oh…" Virtue replied, unconvinced.

While Dale was distracted by Bum's questions about different components of the chicken soup he was eating, Virtue turned to Benny.

"He's lying about Nadia. I'll explain later," Virtue whispered.

Benny became worried. He knew Virtue's foresight was rarely wrong. Had Dale really changed, or had some of his evil leaked through and taken itself out on Nadia? Benny was still skeptical about Bum, but Virtue didn't seem worried about it, so Benny hoped for the best.

Jack noticed Dale and hobbled over to greet him. He introduced Jack to Bum and began describing their adventures in Juvia. Nap, who looked confused, asked where Juvia was, despite hearing Dale mention it earlier.

"I didn't think I'd be giving a geography lesson," Dale said, obviously annoyed, "Okay, sit down guys. As you know, we live in Gant, which is in the Country of Dan. The capital or capitals of this country are the two cities Galver and Elim Dorn, which many refer to as the Sisters Dorn. Now, Juvia is a country to the east of Dan, on the coast. Both are a part of Lower Sultry, which is the continent we live in. Lower Sultry was once a unified Empire which had seceded from Upper Sultry many centuries ago. For a long time there was an Emperor of Lower Sultry, as there is now in Upper Sultry, but over time, more and more land was divided between the various descendants, and eventually the land was split into so many different kingdoms, that the old Empire of Lower Sultry became virtually nonexistent."

"And Duke Dijon of Galver Dorn is the direct descendant of the Emperor's lineage?" Benny asked, remembering old school history lessons.

"It's an accepted truth that Dijon and the Sisters Dorn are the last of the true Lower Sultry Empire, but there is no proof of that. Dijon is the closest thing to a ruler any of the kingdoms of Lower Sultry has, so it's understandable. Anyway, the south became divided more and more by the descendants of the old imperial lineage, and these in turn were damaged by countless civil wars, skirmishes and the like. So, now, aside from Dan, Juvia and a few other larger countries, Lower Sultry is a conglomeration of duchies, earldoms, free cities and independent counties. Trying to maintain some form of pride, a lot of these small principalities have very elaborate names, despite the fact that some of these countries are no bigger than this town. It's ridiculous. This is the main reason the Empire of Upper Sultry and its inhabitants see us southerners as a bunch of hicks and inbred yokels."

"Wow…I didn't know any of that. I only knew of Dan and Ken, where I'm from. I know Ken is south of Dan, but that's as far as my geography goes."

"There's nothing shameful in that. The only reason I know so much is because I've traveled to so many different places." Dale shrugged and bit into a leg of turkey.

Just then there was a loud bang as a group of even stranger men entered the Inn. Benny noticed their odd attire, which consisted of turbans and sashes of bright colors, half-moon and star ornaments hanging from their clothes and weapons. They had very dark complexions, and while they appeared human, many of them had tusks jutting out of their upper jaws. The only one who looked completely human was one smaller man, dressed in tight fitting red and white leather armor. He walked funny, as if he had some sort of deformity, and wore a red hoodie over all his face except for his mouth. The hoodie was embroidered to look like a rat's face. His visible mouth was mottled with pimples and he only had two upper front teeth, which stuck out in an overbite. He had a long strip of white and red silk trailing from the back of his belt. On his back were two curved scimitars. He was obviously the leader of the group. They forced a group of drunkards to leave their table at the other end of the dining hall and began making demands for food and drink. Jack left to see they were appeased, as he had no desire for trouble if it could be avoided.

"Who are those brutes?" Nap asked. Benny shrugged,

and Virtue, who knew quite a bit about the inhabitants of Dan and the surrounding lands was at a loss. Even Dale wasn't sure.

"They're Kudgels," Bum said, "They are the products of centuries of human and orc interbreeding. Roughly five hundred years ago a small band of orc and human pacifists fled Lower Sultry to get away from some civil war, but I don't remember which one. They were shunned for being cowards, and were driven far into the western deserts. They remained a small settlement of mixed breeds, but because of their environment they became very vicious hunters and scavengers. Then, about a century ago, their numbers began to grow considerably. They began moving east into Lower Sultry and converted many peoples to their tribe – usually misfits and vagabonds cast out of society – and I've heard word from some of my cousins in the west that they are building some sort of secret army."

"Are they going to try and take over or something?" Benny asked.

"The larger their numbers grow, the more the odds would lean in their favor," Dale said this time, "They are very warlike, and have a very complex military and social hierarchy. They name their ranks after extinct creatures that at one time lived in this continent. Those men there call themselves ghouls, the equivalent to the common foot soldier. That man in the hood is named Red Rat Flack. I've never met him, but Bum and I have heard stories about him. They say he is the leader of an entire regiment, and worse than that, one of their assassins. Those red and white colors represent his rank, which I think they call the Grand Cerberus."

"But above him are even higher ranking Kudgels. From

what I've heard of these men, they are powerful wizards and warlocks. The highest rank of the Kudgel society, as far as I know, is the Grand Exalted Cyclops. This figure may not even exist, but many people who have studied the Kudgels think he is a wizard of almost infinite power, and maybe not even a true Kudgel by blood, but a convert who ascended the ranks and killed the former leader. He's most likely human, since humans have historically had a better control over magic." Bum finished his speech.

"You two seem to know quite a bit about these men," Virtue said.

"We haven't exactly been hired to 'study' them, but several of our clients in Lower and Upper Sultry think there is a huge conspiracy going on. Dijon claims he has spies in the Kudgel society that verify they are planning to overthrow the governments of Lower Sultry and maybe even Upper Sultry. Bum and I have been forming a network of allies just in case there is any truth to these matters. But, there is no immediate concern. Bum and I just like to be aware of what's happening on the larger scale. I wouldn't worry about it until they start causing serious trouble."

"Oh, the man who threatened to rip out my intestines and choke me with them says there's nothing to worry about. I can sleep easy in my bed tonight." Nap rolled his eyes and walked off to the kitchen for more orders.

"Well, I'd like to stay and chat, but I've got to earn my keep." Virtue kissed Benny and went to help Jack take customers' orders. Benny stayed with Dale and told him about his training with Jack and about his taking over of the more serious duties of the Fox Den.

"Well, Bum and I are taking a few months off of our travels, so we'll stay and help you," Dale told Benny, "and I'll show you some more advanced fighting techniques. Jack's nobody to laugh at, but he hasn't seriously used a sword in so long I'd risk saying his skills aren't what they used to be."

"Yeah, I noticed. I've helped him stay in shape, but I don't think he'll be able to do serious training much longer. He'll be fifty in a month," Benny said.

"Fifty? Old Jack? Wow, time certainly does fly. I'm only forty-two, but I feel twice as old. I can imagine how Jack feels." Dale laughed.

Just then Benny heard a loud voice coming from the Kudgels who had just sat down. He would've let it pass through one ear and out the other, but he saw Virtue standing near the man Dale called Red Rat Flack.

"You think I want to drink watered-down hog's piss?" The man threw a pint of ale on Virtue. Benny stood up and walked towards them. He knew Virtue could handle the man, but he didn't want to risk his wife getting hurt.

"If you like, I can get you something else. We have some nice cider," Virtue was gritting her teeth, trying to be polite.

"No cider tonight, but I might take a bite outa that fine dumper you got there!" Flack slapped Virtue on the butt so hard she lurched forward and spilled the remaining ale she carried all over herself.

Oh no he didn't! Benny thought. Virtue looked at him, almost as if reading his mind, and winked at him. Benny knew what would happen. Being a pacifist, Virtue never bit an unruly customer in a way that would inflict permanent damage, but she liked to scare them with a temporary paralysis bite that usually kept men like Flack in line. She bore her fangs, which seemed to surprise Flack, and in an instant she dove to the man's neck and bit him.

"You witch!" he shouted.

Benny was shocked at what happened next. Instead of going stiff and falling out of his chair, Flack pushed Virtue off him and stood up. Virtue clutched her stomach as if sick, and winced in pain.

"What'd you just do to my wife?" Benny screamed, drawing the short sword he kept at his waist and approaching Flack. The man laughed.

"I get bitten by that whore and you have the audacity to get angry at me when she pays the price? I can't help that my blood's poison to vampires!" The entire group of Kudgels laughed hysterically.

Benny rushed to Virtue and held her from falling. "What's wrong?" Benny asked.

"First nausea, then diarrhea and a whole bunch of scrumptious little goodies," Flack said, drawing his scimitars, "But I can put the wench out of her misery if you like!"

He dove at Virtue, and Benny knew he'd never have time to block the swords. Miraculously, a huge spiked club came crashing down on Flack's hands, knocking the scimitars to the floor and breaking one of Flack's hands. Flack screamed in pain and clutched his hand. The Kudgels rose and drew their swords as Dale stood between Virtue and Flack.

"I'd advise you to leave, or I'll kill you and then all your friends," Dale's voice dripped with menace.

"Beranger!" Flack stated. The man clutched his broken hand as he stared at Dale. For a split second, the man's mouth contorted in a look of pure fear before smiling a sly grin.

"The name's Dale if you please," Dale said.

"I was wondering if I'd ever see you again. I guess the

stories about you are true, then," Flack said.

"Stories?" Dale asked.

"You've gone soft, boy. The Beranger I knew and heard of would have killed me and that couple there for disturbing his meal, yet here you are, watching over them like a mother bear nursing her cubs!" Flack laughed.

"You speak as if you know me," Dale said, "Yet I don't recognize your voice. Perhaps if you'd remove that mask you cower under…"

"You'd like to see my face, wouldn't you, Beranger? No, not now. I'm gonna leave…I'm gonna let ya'll think you're safe." A Kudgel ghoul picked up Flack's weapons and they headed for the door. "But when you think you're safe, you're not. We'll meet again."

After the ghouls and Flack left, Dale and Bum helped Benny carry a worsening Virtue to their bedroom. Things didn't look good.

CHAPTER 4

Virtue's sickness came and went over the next few days, and each time it relapsed it seemed worse than before. Bum made some special tea, which he claimed they used for many ailments in his tribe. While it kept Virtue from getting any worse, it didn't stem the coming and going of the infection entirely.

"His blood tasted like death," she said one day, "I've never encountered anything like that before. It felt as if my body was about to fall apart."

"I should've warned you about the Kudgels. Dale told me you were a vampire, but I didn't know the inn's policy about what happens when men slap your buttocks," Bum said. Benny, who was sitting near Virtue on the edge of their bed, looked at the orc.

"What about the Kudgels?" Benny asked.

"In order to help them survive in the harsh desert environment, they do all manner of things to their bodies in case they are attacked by various creatures. One thing they do is inject chemicals into their bloodstream which act as a poison for vampires and other types of blood sucking creatures. I don't know what it is, or how to cure it, but

I've heard it can be deadly. My herbal tea seems to have stopped the bacteria from Flack's blood from progressing, but it didn't take it away. I'm afraid you're at a stalemate. You won't get better, but at least you won't get worse."

"Thank you for all your help, Bum," Virtue said, holding his hand and kissing it. Benny shook the orc's hand as well.

"Yes, Bum. Thank you," Benny stated.

"Don't mention it. There's nothing I enjoy more than helping those in need."

Dale was standing at the window of Benny's room, rapping his fingers on the window sill. He then began to pace back and forth across the room, a worried look on his face. "This isn't good. From what I know of Flack, which isn't much, he's not the type of man to forgive and forget. I have a feeling we haven't seen the last of him or the Kudgels. But, the strangest thing is that he seemed to know me from somewhere. He's human, I could tell, but I have no recollection of even being in the same vicinity as he or his band."

"Perhaps we should stay here for a while," Bum said, "and watch out for him."

"Look, I appreciate it, but Jack and I are more than capable of protecting the Fox Den," Benny said, drawing his sword and swiping it through the air for emphasis.

Dale wasn't impressed. "There's no telling how many Kudgels are in this area, and if Flack is the Grand Cerberus, then there could be an infinite number of them at his disposal. He'd sic his dogs on this place just for the hell of it."

"Jack and I can handle them," Benny stated.

"Jack's too out of shape, and while I don't doubt your fighting skills have improved significantly, you're still not good enough with a sword to defend against dozens, maybe even hundreds of those Kudgel ghouls," Dale said, "Bum and I are experienced with fighting larger numbers. We'll stay here for a while and protect Gant. We have contacts all over Lower Sultry who will arise if there is a mass invasion. For now, it would seem the Kudgels are merely trying to stir up trouble."

"Well, I'll help you if it comes to a fight," Benny said.

"The Kudgels are like wolves in the night," Bum said. "If they strike, it will be at a time when nobody else expects it."

"Bum and I will teach you some more advanced sword fighting techniques," Dale said. "Hand to hand won't do much against Kudgels."

"When do we start?" Benny sheathed his sword and placed his hands on his hips.

"Why not now?" Bum asked.

"I don't see why not," Dale said, "Change into something more comfortable and we'll meet you in the clearing."

The two men walked out while Benny changed into an outfit more fit for training. Then he remembered what Virtue had mentioned about Nadia, and he addressed the issue again. Virtue laughed and sat up.

"Don't worry, Benny. It's not what you think. He lied because he was embarrassed...Nadia left him for a younger man." Virtue was still laughing.

"You read his mind?" Benny asked, astonished.

"Yes. I'm getting better at it. And no, he doesn't harbor any ill will towards either of them. He's just upset, that's all."

Benny gave her a kiss after changing. "You always amaze me."

They stood in the clearing where Jack sparred with Benny. They'd piled their real weapons off to the side and used the wooden training swords that Benny was used to. Dale had taken his shirt off completely, and Bum was donning the same green tunic he'd worn when Benny first met him. Dale had lost a considerable amount of muscle since Benny fought him, but he was still in great shape, and Benny knew that if anything, Dale's lean physique would improve the man's speed. Benny wondered why Dale had put his fake face back on.

"So, show me what you've learned." Dale raised his sword.

Benny raised his too, assuming a fighting stance. He spread his weight equally on his two legs, and the two fighters slowly began to circle each other. Benny knew not to rush Dale; that's how he'd gotten his own scar. However, Benny knew not to let Dale make the first move. He checked Dale, faking a couple attacks before coming in with a hard thrust to the midsection. He followed with a flurry of blows, all of which Dale easily blocked. Benny then attacked with an overhead strike. In what seemed like one move, Dale blocked the overhead blow with his sword, parried, and allowed his sword to slide out of the block and brought the sword down on Benny's collarbone. It stung, but didn't hurt. Had it been a real fight, Benny would be dead.

"Again," Dale said.

They had several quick bouts, all of which ended with Dale nailing Benny off a counter. Dale never outright attacked Benny, but rather allowed Benny to make mistakes with his attacks that Dale worked off of.

"Now, let me see your defense," Dale said, this time

being the one to attack. He kept his attacks paced out at first, all of which Benny blocked. But his counters were slow and off aim, and Dale came in behind his counters and got him.

"Your offense and defense are good, but you need to work on counter attacking."

"I'm ok. I just need more practice."

"No amount of practice will help that flailing," Bum said, laughing.

"When you block, it needs to be done in such a way that a counter attack can be easily made. They need to flow together, so that they are almost one motion. This is what I like to call a one-step counter attack." Dale had Benny do the overhead blow that Dale "killed" him with the first time. He slowed down this time, though, so Benny could see the motions of the block and counter.

"See what he means?" Bum asked. Benny nodded.

"This can be very useful when fighting Kudgels. Remember, we have no firsthand experience, but we've done lots of research, talked to people who have fought them, and fought similar enemies. One step countering can be great for dispatching enemies quickly, like the Kudgels, who never attack in groups less than a dozen or so. Bum and I will attack you in succession. Remember the block and counter I showed you? I want you to form your own from our attacks. Every blow can be countered…you just need to find it. Bum and I will be screaming and cursing when we attack, since we've heard the Kudgels use noise to intimidate and throw off their opponents."

"You haven't shown me any counters yet!" Benny protested.

"No counter is going to be the same. I showed you one, now you need to figure it out."

Benny closed his eyes and took a deep breath. When he opened them again, Dale and Bum were standing about 10 feet away. Dale came charging in, followed by Bum, whose voice cut through the air with an undulating wail. Dale attacked with a simple slash, aimed at Benny's neck and collarbone on the right side. Benny parried as he blocked the blow to the left, which allowed his sword free air to immediately cut across Dale's chest. Dale gave a fake scream and fell, as the wailing Bum came at Benny, stabbing his sword at Benny. Benny side stepped as he brought his sword down on the orc's hands and followed with a swipe at Bum's neck that would have decapitated him if Benny hadn't been wielding a wooden sword. Bum coughed and grabbed his neck.

"The boy's a quick learner," Bum said.

"That's good. Let's keep going," Dale said.

They continued running different scenarios for the rest of the morning, and after an hour or so they were all sweating profusely, if you could call the green slime oozing from Bum's pores sweat. They grabbed their gear and walked into the dining hall to cool off. They sat down at the rainbow gnome table, and Dale looked around at the walls.

"I've always enjoyed the frescoes on the walls. I see a painting of the Sky Titans over there." Dale pointed to a painting of blue skinned men with aqua green hair falling from a castle suspended in the clouds.

"I've seen that painting my whole life, but never knew who they were. Who are they?" Benny asked.

"They were the first beings that the Protector created in this world. They were to watch over everything else that would be created after them. After the humans, elves, dwarves and other intelligent races began to turn against the Protector, the Sky Titans gave up on the world and moved their castles into the sky. Before they left, though, they built two massive horns. One made of gold, the other of silver. The purpose of these was so that if the world was overtaken by evil, the golden horn could be blown to summon the Sky Titans, who would destroy the world. If the golden horn is blown by mistake, the silver horn is to be blown to let the Sky Titans know the summoning was a false alarm." Dale shrugged.

"That's just a story though, right?" Benny asked.

"Well," Dale pointed at the multi-colored gnomes on the wall behind him, "I thought these fellows were just a story too. Turns out every myth has some truth behind it. Where there's smoke, there's bound to be fire."

Benny noticed for the first time the huge bite marks that wrapped around his entire midsection. The holes were at least two inches in diameter, and one of the tooth marks was directly over a now non-existent nipple. Dale saw Benny staring and smiled.

"They're just souvenirs from my fight with Cycleze. It nearly killed me, but I deserved it. We all reap what we sow," Dale said. Benny wanted to ask for more details, but decided to wait until Dale was ready.

Dale was wiser and more intelligent than Benny had thought he was. Benny was starting to see the man hidden behind the sadistic, uncaring sociopath that had been Beranger. The evil was still a part of Dale; both Benny and Dale knew that. But Benny was starting to view Dale as more than a friend…Dale was becoming family.

Chapter 5

When Benny woke up the next morning Virtue was gone. Hearing some commotion outside, Benny threw on a shirt and leggings and ran outside to find Virtue, Dale, Bum, Jack, and many of the townsfolk huddled in a mass, looking at something in front of the dining hall of the Fox Den. Virtue saw him; her face was grim.

"You need to see this, dear," she said.

"What's going on?" Benny asked.

Pushing his way between Dale and Jack, Benny gasped at what he saw. Scattered in the pathway leading to the Gant village were the remnants of the horse and wagon Dale and Bum had ridden in. The horse had been torn to shreds, with its entrails strewn about the entire mess like a devilish party streamer. The horse's head was spiked onto a shard of wood from the wagon and stuck in the very center of the massacre. Someone had drawn a crude eye symbol on the gray hair of its forehead in coagulated blood.

"What in the Protector's name?!" Benny was too shocked for words.

"Our friend, Flack," Bum said, "That eye is a symbol used by the Kudgel army."

"Why an eye?" asked Nap, who was standing in the crowd.

"It represents their leader, the Grand Exalted Cyclops," Dale said. "The real Cyclopes are now extinct creatures of immense strength and power who are said to have ruled and were worshiped as gods by the intelligent races. They use the name and the symbol to instill fear into their enemies," Dale said.

"They certainly aren't shy about doing it, are they?" Virtue asked.

"This is the first time Bum or I have ever witnessed their handiwork first hand. It has to be Flack. He's still pissed about the other night, and from the way he talked, I assume I did something else to him that he holds a grudge from, which I can't remember." Dale looked confused, "I'm gonna miss ol' Betsy, though. She was a good horse."

"May she graze in greener pastures." Bum laid a hand on Dale's shoulder to comfort him. *Is Dale that upset over a horse?* Benny thought. The man had changed.

The next few weeks, things were relatively uneventful, aside from Benny's advanced training with Dale and Bum. Benny got an eyeful of female body parts when a group of Amazon warrior women passed through Gant. Their home was in the jungles of the deep south, beyond the kingdoms of Lower Sultry, and the border of the known world. They were unnaturally muscular women, who were all scantily clad; some even being naked except for a sword or crudely made crossbow. They were scarred, had many piercings, and some wore face paint and tattoos. Most were shaved bald, but the ones who weren't had their hair in long matted dreadlocks.

Virtue saw Benny staring as he filled the trough for

horses, and slapped him playfully in the back of the head. "You don't want any part of them, dear. They're brutish warriors and sociopaths. They care only for themselves, and I doubt they would let a man as ugly as you become one of their male concubines."

"Virtue, you know you're the only woman I'll ever need." Benny laughed.

"One of the vampires in my old coven had experience with Amazons. They employed vampires to give them berserker bites for various civil wars and for mercenary work. It became dangerous, though. Somehow they learned to control the berserker and healing bites at will. They're only human as far as I know, but they're the only ones I know of who can reverse any and all of the vampire bites. We can't even convert them to vampirism if we wanted to." Virtue ended her monologue abruptly when she clutched her stomach in pain.

"What's wrong?" Benny asked.

"Just what that Flack creep did. It's not getting worse though, don't worry." There was uneasiness in her voice, as if she were hiding something. "There was something in his mind, something that occurred between him and Dale in the distant past. I couldn't read it all, but Dale did something to him. Dale doesn't remember Flack, and I've noticed he's having a hard time remembering the past in general. I think memory loss is an unavoidable side effect of the conversion bite I gave him."

"Better memory loss than having 'Beranger' among us again," Benny said. Virtue silently agreed.

A week later something even stranger happened. Two finely clad boys holding trumpets burst into the Fox Den one night, blowing a lively tune as a man followed them. He was dressed in a full set of bronze armor, a wide brimmed hat, and a cape. He held out a scroll and read aloud to everyone who was sitting in the dining hall.

"I, royal messenger of the Emperor of Upper Sultry, Son of the Sun, hereby invite all worthy fighters to attend a royal tournament in the Imperial City precisely two months from now. The bouts are to be non-lethal. Any murder during a bout will be met with the severest punishment. The winners of the tournament will earn a royal feast with the Emperor himself, and will be allowed to choose a prize, which will include, but are not limited to, the right for a male victor to marry the Emperor's daughter, the right for a female victor to marry one of the Emperor's sons, an entire chest of gold and jewels, a mansion and two servants in Upper Sultry. This said in the name of the Son of the Sun."

The boys blew another tune on their horns and followed the unemotional man out of the room. The room was silent for a moment before the men, women, elves, and dwarves erupted in laughter and making fun of the messenger from Upper Sultry. Benny and Virtue sat at a table with Dale and Bum, and they all looked to each other.

"I think it'd do you some good to travel into Upper Sultry, Ben," Dale said. "It's a beautiful country…closest thing to paradise in this world, though not without its faults. I know some people there you might like to meet."

"I can't just leave the Fox Den and Jack," Benny said.

A hand came down on Benny's shoulder and made him jump. "You and the boys have given me a good amount of rest these last few weeks, Benny," Jack said. "You've helped me long enough. Go, compete, and enjoy your life."

"But what use do I have to fight in a tournament? I

don't need to get married again, and I don't need any gold or a house. I have everything I need here," Benny lied, trying to sound humble.

"Oh, you're worse at concealing the truth than I am," Bum said, "You don't have to compete, but it'd be a fun experience."

"It also might keep Flack and the Kudgels away from the Fox Den…away from Jack and our family," Virtue whispered into his ear.

"What are you going to do if I go with Dale and Bum?" he asked Virtue.

"Take her with us," Dale said, "Her sickness is not bad, aside from some stomach cramps, crapping and vomiting; she should be fine to travel a bit. To travel to Upper Sultry by foot or wagon would take months, and the tournament would be long over before we even got to the border. There's an old teleportation station in a country north of Dan, in Bluecorn Betty. It's the main means of transportation to Upper Sultry. It'll take a week to get there if we hurry, and about a week to get to the Imperial City once we get in Upper Sultry. We'll have enough time to stay with a friend of mine before going to fight."

"You mean old Purp?" Bum said, smiling. Benny didn't know who they were talking about, but assumed it was a close friend of Dale's.

"Yep, that's him." Dale turned to Benny. "If you thought I was a handful when you and I first met, you'll love him."

CHAPTER 6

The next day Dale, Bum the orc, Benny and Virtue set out from the Fox Den. Jack had gone that morning and borrowed a wagon with a built-in cabin, and a mule, from his distant cousin the blacksmith. The cabin had only three cots, Benny and Virtue sharing one while Dale and Bum took the others.

They left Gant without any trouble and made for Galver Dorn. The quartet didn't get started until midday, and by the time they made it to the giant's pass, where Dale killed the giant Kidneywart, they decided it was best to pack it in for the night and visit Liverwart. The wagon wouldn't fit through the trees, and rather than stay in the uncomfortable cabin, they decided to sleep in Liverwart's fortress.

The giant was glad to see them all, and quickly introduced Benny and Virtue to his wife, who was even larger than he was, and their five year old son, who was already as tall as Benny. Being a giant, the child had gangly, disproportioned limbs and a distended gut. Both he and his mother wore loin cloths, while Liverwart tried to dress more modestly (most likely an inherited trait from working in Gant).

"Who's this little fella?" Virtue asked, pointing to the child-giant. Liverwart smiled proudly and placed a hand on his son's shoulder.

"Me son, Picklewart."

"Nice to meet you, Pickle!" Benny said.

He held out a hand to the child-giant, who looked at him confusedly. Picklewart then pulled a booger out of his nose and ate it. Liverwart's eyes grew wide and he smacked his son on the back of the head, chastising him in their own tribal dialect. The giant then looked at the quartet and gave an embarrassed chuckle.

"He shy." The boy was going to town eating more boogers as his father spoke.

"Or just hungry." Bum laughed.

"You stay night?" Liverwart asked.

"If you'll have us," said Dale.

The giant said nothing, but instead jumped up and down with glee, shaking the ground around them. He showed them into the fortress that had belonged to his cousin, Kidneywart. He had removed all the skeletons and garbage that the former giant had placed in the keep, and had built some modest looking furnishings. Liverwart had even built some human-sized beds for guests. Benny noticed out of the corner of his eye Liverwart whispering into his son's ear and pointing at Benny.

"Oh no," Benny exclaimed.

"What?" Virtue asked.

"Wrestle! Wrestle!" The giant-child lumbered towards Benny.

Benny remembered how Liverwart used to wrestle with Jack, many times nearly ripping the man in half. He thought his superior speed would keep him away from Picklewart, but no such luck. The boy moved with incredible agility, catching Benny by the wrist and ankle in one motion, picking him up and throwing the man to the ground. Then he fell right on top of Benny's prone form. The kid had to weigh almost three hundred pounds, and Benny barely broke two hundred. Benny used all his might to try to wiggle out from under Picklewart, but all the giant had to do was keep the bulk of his weight on Benny's chest. Liverwart's proud laughter could be heard echoing off the sapling-walls of the fortress.

"Okay…about…all I can…do now…is wait till …this oaf …gets off me!" Benny gasped.

"Pickle, off!" Liverwart yelled, and the kid-giant laughed and stood up, immediately sticking his pointer finger back into his nose.

"Don't feel bad, Benny. Mountain giants have the strength of a full grown human by the time they're toddlers." Dale helped Benny up.

"I have an idea…" Virtue then whispered something in Benny's ear.

"Yes! That's a great idea, honey!"

Benny tilted his head to the side as Virtue leaned in to kiss, and at the last minute lightly biting him just under the jaw line. Benny could feel the blood pumping through his veins and into his muscles as the strength bite did its magic.

"Round two?" Benny asked Picklewart.

"Wrestle!" The giant rushed in.

This time, Benny caught both the giant's wrists before he was thrown a second time. Picklewart struggled to overpower Benny, but quickly realized their strength was now equal. Instead of getting upset, though, the lad appeared more excited to have a challenge. They proceeded to attempt throws and takedowns on each other. The match spilled to the ground where they grappled until Benny managed to catch Picklewart's head in a leg-scissors lock. Benny squeezed his thighs, cutting off air into the giant's enormous head until it tapped Benny's leg, signaling the human had won. It was a good thing, too, because Virtue's strength bite was just starting to wear off.

"How you strong now?" Picklewart asked.

Benny and Virtue winked at each other, and Liverwart, who knew of Virtue's bites, giggled as he put a hand on his son's shoulder.

"Humans stronger than you think," Liverwart stated.

They appreciated each other's company, and enjoyed a huge feast prepared by the giantess, who despite her lack in clothing was not lacking in proper dinner-time etiquette. The quartet slept until the next morning. They awoke, took care of nature's business, and started on the road to the country of Bluecorn Betty and the transportation portal to Upper Sultry.

They didn't stay long in Galver Dorn; in fact they didn't technically enter the city. Dale was eager to get away from the place, knowing that if Dijon realized he was there he and Bum would be harassed about doing more work. Instead, they visited a few of the vendors in the market outside the main city, and bought some produce for the next day's journey. Once they left, they encountered mostly flatland forests and cow pastures.

"So what is this portal thing?" Benny asked.

"There used to be tons of them all over the world," Virtue explained. "Some ancient civilization used them as a means of quick and instant transportation to different locations all over the kingdoms."

"As of now, there are only two still known to function," Dale said. "This one, obviously, is in Bluecorn Betty; the other is in the middle of a field in Upper Sultry. There are many ruins of portals scattered throughout Lower and Upper Sultry, but they are long since defunct."

"Technically the portal we are going to isn't even in Bluecorn Betty, but an even smaller country, which is actually the bell tower of Bluecorn Castle," Bum said. "They call it Siegfried's Bell, and it only consists of the tower, portal, and a small living quarters for the wizard who operates the portal."

"An entire sovereign nation contained in a section of a castle in another country?" Virtue asked, confused by Bum's explanation.

"Yes. It's quite stupid, but they're recognized as two separate nations." Bum shrugged.

"It'll be the first time I've been out of Dan, so I'm excited to see it," Benny said.

Once night fell, they pulled the wagon off into a clearing and slept, with Bum and Dale trading places guarding the other travelers. They did this for two more days, passing through several smaller settlements until finally reaching a small wooden sign marking the boundaries of Dan. They spent another day traveling through an unclaimed section of land until nighttime, where their path reached a thick forest with an almost unnoticeable sign saying they were entering the Sovereign Nation of Bluecorn Betty.

"What's with the name?" Virtue asked. Dale, being the unofficial geographer of the voyage, was quick to respond.

"There was a family of farmers led by this old woman named Betty. They found the ruins of an old castle and turned it into a settlement. Their harvest was a rare type of blue corn, which the family became famous for. That same family and a few other settlers are the only actual citizens of the country. They are mainly a checkpoint for travelers."

They traveled through the forest until they came to a huge structure illuminated by some kind of magical light. It was the ruins of a stone castle that had been built on a huge rock base. Benny was shocked to see that the actual township of the castle was literally built onto the ruins, which consisted of several layers of boardwalks and wooden buildings of a similar architecture to the township of Gant. At the very top of the castle, on the highest tower, was what looked like a small stone cottage spiked through the highest parapet. Benny squinted and saw a couple men walk up a ladder, into the cottage, and a burst of light shot out the windows.

"Somebody just teleported," Bum said.

"This place is kinda cool," Virtue said.

"Yep, but all kinds of scum pass through here, so stick together," Dale said.

They pulled the wagon up to a man with a torch, who, after Dale explained their destination, accepted a hefty sum to watch the mule until the quartet returned. They walked around to the side of the rocky base of the castle, and Benny gasped, surprised to see a cave dug into it. There was a stone staircase winding along its wall, and was evidently the entrance into the castle-town. A huge elm grew under a strange crystalline orb at the top of the cave ceiling, and underneath the tree there was a small pool. Before walking up into the town, Dale stood by the pool and whistled. The water of the small pond rippled, and the form of a woman erupted out of the waters. She was made almost completely of water, and her naked form walked up to Dale and kissed him on the cheek. However, it was quickly obvious by the way the water spirit treated Dale that they had a mother and son relationship rather than that of lovers. He called her 'mama,' and gave her one last kiss before she returned to the water.

"Her home pond dried up, and I transported her here." Dale laughed. "She thinks she's my mother."

"Poor thing, having a son like you…" Virtue chided.

"She can't talk, at least not the way we can. Her race is almost extinct…I always say hi to her when I pass through here. It'd hurt her feelings if I didn't," Dale said, walking towards the stairway.

Benny smiled at how much Dale had changed. The fact that he not only helped the water spirit, but continued to play along with its 'mother-son' charade, revealed the man's dire need for companionship.

"You guys coming?" Virtue called to Benny, who had remained standing at the pond.

There were three levels of the town, the lowest being the market, the second being an Inn and tavern, and the highest being Siegfried's Bell and the portal to Upper Sultry. Virtue asked several of the farmers in the market about some strange fruit they were selling, and then the group headed to the tavern and inn for a meal and some sleep. The tavern was built onto the side of the ruins, and the inn rooms had been built into the inner structure of the old castle. Upon entering, Benny was greeted by the smell of tobacco smoke, liquor, and roasted meat. A tall, lanky man with short hair and missing his earlobes walked over to Dale. He had a sour look on his face and when he reached the group he angrily motioned towards Bum and Virtue.

"Get outta here and take these two with you! We don't want their kind here!" He was fuming.

Dale seemed shocked that the man was acting like this, and then felt his face, realizing, as Benny had, that he'd been wearing his prosthetic face for the entire journey thus far. He peeled it off, and the man's demeanor quickly changed.

"Beranger, you devil! Why didn't you say it was you?" He hugged Dale and looked at Bum and Virtue. "I'm sorry I was so harsh, but we've had bad experience with vampires and orcs. But, if you're friends of Dale, you're friends of mine."

Dale and the skinny man, whom they learned was named Marty Danaher, told a few quick jokes, laughed and slapped each other's backs as they walked to a booth in the far corner. They all sat down and the man scratched his hooked nose as Dale told him about their trek to the tournament.

"Yeah, some puffy prancing pony waltzed in here too with a similar message. I ain't got no use for fighting in no tournament…being a bouncer is tough enough," Marty said.

"Marty here is the best fist-fighter in all of Lower Sultry!" Dale exclaimed, "He's so good, he doesn't even need weapons."

"That's a bit of an exaggeration, but I'll take it." Marty rubbed a bruise under his eye.

"Where'd you get the shiner?" Bum asked. The man giggled and took a sip of beer from a mug he'd apparently been holding the whole time.

"Some Amazons passed through here on their way to that tournament. One of them tried to get frisky with me and when I didn't reciprocate she got pissed and started hitting me. Her and her lot put up a good fight, but they were drunk and me and my boys took care of them. We sent them right on their way to Upper Sultry." Marty leaned back and continued to scratch his nose.

"We need some rooms for the night. We've been traveling the last week and need a night of comfort before teleporting to Upper Sultry. Can you help out an old friend?" Dale asked.

The man frowned. "Well, ya'll can eat here, and maybe you and the boy can get some rooms, but the boss may not take kindly to an orc and vampire sleeping over. Let me check." Marty stood up and walked into a crowd of patrons.

"I'll go get some drinks," Benny said, standing up and going to the bar.

The bartender fixed them three mugs of non-alcoholic cider (Dale didn't like to drink while doing extensive traveling) and one mug of a mint tea that the bartender suggested Benny try. The man seemed a bit eager for Benny to try the tea, but Benny didn't think anything of it. As he walked back to his booth, he thought he noticed a man in a striped shirt staring at him from across the room, but he quickly shook it off. Marty had returned as well.

"Oh, Benny is it? I was just telling Dale that I talked the boss into letting you, Dale and the orc have rooms, but he doesn't want anything to do with your wife…I might be able to sneak her in, though…" He shrugged.

"That won't be necessary, Mr. Danaher. I understand your boss's discrepancies," Virtue said, "I'll ask the nice fruit vendor in the market sector if she could spare a room. If not, don't worry about me."

"Are you sure?" Marty asked.

"Yes. I don't want to start any trouble. I'll just meet

back up with the others at the portal in the morning."

"Whatever." Marty left to prevent a rising argument between two dwarves that might have resulted in a brawl.

"What're you drinking there Ben?" Dale asked.

"Some mint tea the bartender told me to try. Why?"

"Nothing, just curious."

Dale and Bum looked at each other and glanced around the room suspiciously. Benny shook it off and took his first sip of the tea. It was extremely sweet and aromatic, warming him from his head all the way to his toes. Benny began to get very giddy all of a sudden, but after he finished his tea he began to grow extremely tired.

"What's wrong, honey? You look like you're about to pass out." Virtue put a hand on Benny's shoulder to steady him. Dale whispered something into Virtue's ear, but Benny didn't notice.

"Well, maybe I'll go ask that lady about a room before it gets late. I'll see you boys in the morning." Virtue kissed Benny and left the tavern.

Dale and Bum hauled a half conscious Benny into his room and helped him take off his traveling clothes and put him in bed. They in turn left to go to their separate rooms. From the shadows of the adjacent corridor, the man who had been watching the scar-faced boy the entire night carefully walked to Benny's door. After silently picking the lock, he pulled a dagger from his belt and entered. Soon, the scarred man would be dead, and the amateur assassin could collect his reward.

CHAPTER 7

It was dark, and the man was nervous and clumsy. But even if he wasn't able to control his breathing, the sleeping potion he bribed the bartender to put in the boy's drink was enough to keep anyone asleep for quite some time. He raised the knife as he hovered over Benny, poised and ready to strike. All of a sudden, there was a cracking noise as a porcelain bed-pan broke over the man's head, porcelain and waste spraying everywhere. Marty Danaher now stood over the unconscious assassin, a crudely rolled cigar sticking out of the corner of his mouth. Dale and Bum entered after him.

"A bedpan, Marty? Really?" Dale laughed.

"Well, I was pinching one off when I heard the guy walking this way and I didn't have time to grab anything else." He kicked at the bits of bedpan.

Dale and Bum quickly wrapped up the unconscious assailant in Benny's bed sheet and then wrapped the cords from the window curtains around him to keep him subdued. The man was chubby and obviously not a trained assassin. His clumsy footsteps that Marty, Dale, and Bum had heard from their rooms were evidence of that. Benny slowly aroused and noticed the three working on securing the man.

"What…" Benny rubbed the sleep out of his eyes.

"Have a nice nap, princess?" Dale asked.

"What happened? Last thing I remember I was drinking that tea…" Benny had a headache.

"I overheard this fella bribing the bartender to slip some sleeping potion into your drink so he could kill you during the night. I told Dale about it, and was gonna tell you but he said not to." Marty shrugged.

"You what?" Benny became angry. "I could've been killed and you just let me walk right into it?"

"Hold your horses, boy!" Dale's face was stern, and Benny knew not to argue with Dale in this state.

"Dale was teaching you a lesson, Ben. You always need to be aware of what's going on around you. I overheard this oaf bribing the bartender and even saw the bartender put the potion in your drink, and I wasn't even standing near him. I made a similar mistake a while back…was partying in a tavern like this, and the next thing I knew, my earlobes were nailed to a tree in a goblin camp. Needless to say, I ripped myself off the tree and escaped, but I wouldn't have had to if I had been paying attention." Marty sat down next to Benny.

"I thought it was a bit strange how the bartender kept insisting I try the mint tea," Benny said.

"That's because the potion he used is less noticeable in that tea," Bum said.

"You've got to pay more attention, Benny," Dale said.

Just then the man began to stir, and then when he realized he was tied up and surrounded by three menacing warriors he began to plead for his life.

"Please don't kill me! Somebody hired me to do it…I

needed the money for my family." The man's chubby face began to sweat.

"Who hired you, and why?" Dale asked.

"I don't know his name, but he was with a group of Kudgels. He wore a red hoodie over his face."

"Flack!" Benny yelled.

"Maybe, I dunno. Anyway, he told me the target was a man with a scarred face. I saw the boy's mouth and assumed it was him. Flack told me to slip some sleeping potion into his drink, break into his room and kill him in his sleep. I paid the bartender to slip in the potion, which the hooded man gave me. He even gave me an enchanted lock pick so I wouldn't fail. I'm sorry! My family is on the brink of starvation and he paid me almost fifteen pieces of silver to do it." The man wiggled with all his might but couldn't get loose.

"That was smart of Flack, hiring this drunkard to do his dirty work," Bum said.

"I ain't no drunk!" the assassin protested.

"Your eyes are bloodshot and your face is red as a beet…besides, I've seen you in the tavern loads of times drinking. Don't give me your sob story." Marty kicked the man in the gut and grabbed the knife the man would have used to kill Benny.

"No, Marty," Dale said. "This guy is a piece of crap, but so were we, once upon a time." Marty dropped the knife, and seemed to agree with Dale's logic.

"There was a time when all three of us did things like what you attempted," Bum motioned to himself, Marty and Dale, "and while we were quite a bit better at it than you, we were all given a chance to turn our lives around. I doubt you'll see the error of your ways, like we did, but perhaps this instance will scare you from attempting murder again."

"I'll leave and never come back!" The man squirmed and kicked frantically. Dale untied him and Marty grabbed him in a headlock, dragging him out of the inn and out into the night.

"Why would Flack want to kill me?" Benny asked.

"I don't think he meant to kill you," Dale said. He raised his hands to his fake face, which he had put back on after meeting Marty upon entering the tavern.

"That face of yours is a charm." Bum laughed. "You're right, Dale. You didn't have that face off long enough for that fat retard to notice, and he obviously assumed Benny was the 'scarred man' Flack told him to kill. That was a mistake on Flack's part…he should've been more specific."

"I'm sorry, Dale. I won't make the same mistake again," Benny said. Dale winked at him and playfully punched Benny on the shoulder.

"Don't apologize to me. You're the one who'll wind up dead." Dale laughed.

Benny could tell Dale's sarcasm was half-hearted, and that Dale had only been angry before because he cared about Benny, and didn't want him doing something to get himself killed. Benny was actually moved by it.

Benny, Dale, and Bum cleaned up the glass and human excrement that had scattered everywhere when Marty broke the bedpan over the assassin's head. Marty returned and told them that he had alerted the boss about what happened and that the bartender was kicked out of the town too. Relieved to finally sleep in peace, Benny dozed off, and Marty stayed with him just in case Flack had hired any more of the village idiots to knock off the 'scarred man.'

Chapter 8

In the morning they got up, cleaned up, bid farewell to Bum and Marty, and went to find Virtue. The moment she saw Benny she read his mind and picked up on the mischief he had suffered after they separated. "I think it is not safe for me to leave you to your own devices," she said. "I had better stay with you after this."

"Please do!" Benny said, kissing her. He knew that she would have been able to shore him up against the sleeping potion. Apart from that, he hated ever being apart from her.

They walked into the inner structure of Bluecorn Castle, a solid stone edifice with an impressive tower in its center that reached up into a cloud that obscured its top. A guard at the entry halted them. "Who are you and what do you want?" he demanded.

"We are here to use the portal," Dale said gruffly. "Siegfried's Belltower."

"It's not open to trespassers."

Dale put his hand on his sword, but Virtue interceded. "We are travelers on legitimate business. I am sure you understand." She kissed him on the cheek.

The guard was evidently stunned by the gesture. "Oh.

Of course. Pass on through."

"There's nothing like the kiss of a fair lady to melt a man's resistance," Dale remarked as they entered the castle. "You bit him, of course?"

"Oh, you caught me," Virtue confessed. "It was just a little nick to make him amenable."

"She could have done it with just the kiss, if necessary," Benny said. "I am putty when she kisses me."

"You're putty anyway," Dale said. "We're trying to cure you of that."

They entered the tower, which was marked TO SIEGFRIED'S BELL. It looked empty, but Dale led the way confidently up the winding stairway to the top, shrouded in mist. As they came to the upper landing a small dwarf appeared. He had purple hair and beard. "Halt!" the dwarf said in a surprisingly loud voice. "This is a private nation."

"We are here to use the portal," Dale repeated. "That is a public access facility, is it not?"

"That depends," the dwarf said belligerently.

Dale touched his sword warningly, as he had before, but Virtue interceded again. "Please," she said beseechingly, and kissed him on the cheek.

The dwarf seemed about to faint, but Virtue steadied him with a hand to his shoulder. "I knew a handsome man like you would be reasonable."

"Did you bite me?" the dwarf demanded.

"I did," Virtue said. "I apologize. It was a token. I did you no harm."

"You put me in heaven for a moment. I've never been touched by a woman, or kissed by one, let alone a lovely creature like you. I wish you'd spend a night in my bed, naked, and bite me all you wanted, as long as I could clasp you."

Benny winced. Had Virtue gone too far this time? The dwarf's sullenness had been replaced by crude passion.

Virtue smiled. "I'm married. My husband wouldn't understand."

"They never do," the dwarf agreed with resignation. "This way, please."

Beyond the landing was the flat top of the tower roof, with the vapor of the cloud seeming like a surrounding landscape. A somewhat dilapidated house was there, as if the roof were the ground. From the center of the building rose the bell tower, supporting a monstrous blue bell.

"Master!" the dwarf called. "Company!"

A white-bearded man appeared, garbed in a tattered robe. He came across more like a sleepy old timer than anyone with the power of magic. Benny wondered if there really was a magic portal. "Did they pay for passage?"

"Not exactly."

The Wizard frowned. "And you let them through?"

"I--" The dwarf seemed to run out of words.

"I kissed him," Virtue said. "I will kiss you too, if that's what it takes to use the portal."

"Ah, a vampire," the Wizard said, as if that explained things. He eyed Virtue. "Poisoned by a villain. Pity; you're a pretty one."

"You wouldn't happen to have a cure?" Benny asked with sudden irrational hope.

"Not my specialty," the Wizard said. He glanced at Dale. "Good to see you again, friend. You brought the fee?"

"What fee, you old rogue?" Dale demanded.

"We rent this property from Bluecorn Betty. It was also a chore assembling the bits and pieces from ruined portals to cobble this one together. How do you think we gain the necessary coin?"

"I thought you conjured it," Dale said.

"Not my specialty."

"What's this about bits and pieces?" Dale demanded. "Isn't a portal a portal, that works or doesn't?"

"It still has to be maintained. We don't want it blowing people up if it doesn't work right."

"Hardy. Har. Har," Dale said. "Very funny. Open a window; I might even have to let out a laugh."

The Wizard drew back, affrighted. "Anything but that! We're still trying to clear the stink of your last laugh."

This had gone on far enough. "We have coin," Benny said.

Dale silenced him with a gesture. "What are you angling for, you ancient reprobate?"

"Your vamp girl kisses well."

Dale was firm. "You can't have her. Stick to your conjured nymphs."

"They won't touch my servant, because of his hair."

"Have you forgotten that you changed his hair when one of your spells went awry? It's your fault."

The Wizard sighed. "Aye, and I have never found the counter-spell. I thought to give him one good night regardless."

Benny and Virtue glared. "Not with her," Dale said quickly.

The Wizard waggled a finger at him. "I know what vamps can do. Stay the night, and I will feed you well and invoke the portal for you in the morning."

"We are in a hurry," Dale said. "That's why we choose to use the portal."

"Time can vary with the individual."

Dale glanced at Virtue. "This seems like a good offer."

"It will do," Virtue said.

"Wait!" Benny cried. "She's not about to--"

Virtue put a soft hand on his arm. "Peace," she murmured.

Benny shut up, though hardly at ease.

The Wizard ushered them into his abode. "Go to your bed," he told the dwarf. "You will have company."

The dwarf obediently went to the small bed nestled under a timber supporting the bell tower. Virtue went and knelt beside him. She leaned forward and gently bit him on the shoulder. The dwarf sank into sleep immediately, smiling.

"It's not that I don't trust you," the Wizard said. "But let me verify before we address the portal."

"As you please," Dale said.

The Wizard gestured. A cloud formed beside the bed, pulsating with its own kind of life. It clarified, forming into a three dimensional picture. Within the picture the dwarf lay on his bed, while a figure strongly resembling Virtue was removing her clothing. Gloriously nude, she went to the bed and got under the blanket with the dwarf.

His eyes popped open, in the picture, though they remained closed in his real life. He reached out to embrace her. She smiled and kissed him on the mouth. Then they both disappeared under the blanket.

"How long will it last?" the Wizard asked the real Virtue.

"About six hours."

"Good enough." The Wizard clapped his hands and the vision disappeared. Only the sleeping dwarf remained, smiling broadly. "That's all night, for him."

Now Benny understood. It was all the dwarf's dream,

sponsored by Virtue's bite. He could have at her fantasy self for six hours, and wake at last with a phenomenal memory. The dream figure would surely oblige anything he could imagine. A unique payment for the use of the portal.

"Go up and sit in the clapper," the Wizard told them. "I will ring the bell from here." He put his hand on a stout rope that dangled down into the room. "Dismount after it clangs thrice. I will see you then."

"Got it," Dale said. "Thank you, Wiz."

"You paid. Let's hope it really doesn't blow you up if it doesn't work right." He smiled to show this was the joke repeated, though Benny wasn't much amused.

Dale glanced at Virtue. "I owe you one."

"You will surely find a way."

Dale believed in the power of the Wizard, and Virtue had faith. Benny was the odd one out.

They climbed the circular stairs. "I didn't know you could do that," Benny told Virtue.

"It was my secret."

He was amazed. "You mean sometimes, when I clasped you--"

"Sometimes the sickness held me, and I did not want to disappoint you."

Benny thought back, trying to distinguish reality from dream, and found that he could not. She had always been there for him. How could he protest?

They came up under the giant bell. There was the clapper hanging in the center. It had seats for three, facing outward from the center.

Benny helped Virtue into one seat, then took one himself. Dale took the third. "Strap in," Dale said. "It may get giddy." He passed around a thick strap that circled them all at low chest height. Then he called down to the Wizard. "Ready!"

The rope attached to the tongue of the clapper drew tight. It drew them to one side, then the other, then back, causing them to swing more widely each time. Benny felt dizzy.

"Cover your ears," Dale told them. They obliged.

Then the outer guard of the clapper struck the shell of the bell. **Bong**! The sound was painfully loud, possibly deafening if they had not kept their ears tightly covered. **Bong! Bong!**

Dale reached out and stopped the clapper from striking the bell again. They dismounted, and made their way down the stairs.

"Nothing has changed," Benny said querulously.

"Oh, it has," Dale said confidently.

Yet they were still in the creaky bell tower, not away to some distant land. What was the point?

Virtue squeezed his hand. She had more faith than he did.

The Wizard remained in the lower chamber. The dwarf still slept in his bed, smiling.

Benny opened his mouth, but Dale silenced him with firm pressure on his elbow. "Thank you, Wizard."

"You're welcome, Dale. Come this way again when your mission is done."

"We may," Dale agreed. Then he opened the door, and they stepped out.

Now Benny opened his mouth again, ready to give Dale a huge piece of his mind. And paused, mouth open.

The town was gone. They faced a virtual paradise of green pastures and a beautiful forest of strange trees. The smell was different, and the temperature.

"I think we're not in Bluecorn Castle anymore," Virtue whispered.

That was certainly true. They were in the fabled land of Upper Sultry.

Benny turned around to glance at the penthouse with its bell tower. He froze again. They were gone. There was only pristine field and forest there.

"You'll get used to it," Dale said jovially. "It's the little details of magic that get to you, more than the magic itself."

Benny wondered when he would ever get used to it. As a child he had seen mostly minor magic, not major magic like this.

A finely dressed human man strode from the lovely forest ahead of them. He was huge, over nine feet tall, but he did not look like the giants Benny had known.

"He's a native of Upper Sultry," Dale explained. "They are not giants, technically, because they have a different muscle and bone structure. They are usually slimmer and not as strong as giants, though some can be just as tall."

As the man approached closer, Benny saw that what he had taken for a suit of clothes was actually finely crafted armor that fit as well as a suit. This was a warrior.

"Hello, travelers!" the man called. "How may I help you?"

At least he was friendly. Benny had seen Dale take down a giant before, but he really didn't want any enemies of that stature.

"We are travelers from the country of Dan," Dale replied. "We took the portal at Bluecorn Betty. We are here to attend the tournament at the Emperor's Palace. Can you point us in the right direction?"

"That way," the man said, pointing. "A fifteen minute walk." Then he reconsidered. "Make that half an hour, for your size."

"Thank you," Dale said.

The man glanced at Virtue. "You're a pretty one. I didn't know vampires were entering the tournament."

"We're not," Virtue said. "I am mainly moral support."

"That's fine." The man walked on.

"He was cautious," Virtue said. "I read his mind. He didn't quite trust us, until I sent reassurance."

"That's because of past history," Dale said. "The several nations and species are at peace now, but that was not always the case. Not that long ago, Sultry was a unified nation roughly divided into two provinces. Upper Sultry's citizens were like that man we just met, powerful and proud. They saw the denizens of Lower Sultry as a bunch of backwoods hicks, though that was unfair; they were less adventurous but had talents of their own. There were incidents, such as a lynching that was blamed on the Lower Sultrians, and passions led to war. Neither side prevailed, but the two provinces became two nations who remain vaguely hostile to this day. When it became clear that we were not Lower Sultrians, our border guard was reassured. For one thing, there are no vampires here; the only intruders are Amazons, who can take care of themselves."

"They certainly can," Virtue said. "I don't like Amazons."

Benny was surprised. Virtue was generally tolerant of all other peoples. Why did she make an exception for Amazons? Now he remembered how she had spoken ill of them when a contingent passed through Gant, calling them dangerous mercenaries. It seemed that the vampires and

Amazons had interacted at one point, and evidently parted ways less than amicably.

"It's complicated," Virtue murmured, picking up his thought. "Nothing you need be concerned about."

All the same, Benny hoped they did not encounter any Amazons.

"Now I recognize the terrain," Dale said. "I have a house here. We'll stay there."

"A house?" Benny asked. "I thought you were a chronic wanderer."

"I am. But I rescued a nobleman from a highwayman during my travels around the realm, and he insisted on rewarding me with a place to stay in comfort. So when I am here, I use it, as a matter of courtesy."

"I'm glad there will be a place," Virtue said. "I am tired."

Benny looked at her. She had become downright peaked. "The illness?" he asked.

"It comes and goes, but is getting worse. I fear I am in for a nasty siege."

Bunny realized that she must have felt it coming on before, but not mentioned it so as not to inhibit him. "You must rest, yes," he said.

They emerged from the forest. There ahead was a phenomenal mansion.

"Ah, my house," Dale said.

Benny exchanged a glance and thought with Virtue. Some house!

But it was surely a good place for Virtue to rest.

CHAPTER 9

They walked along the curving drive toward the mansion, through elegantly tailored gardens with decorative statuary. It was evident that someone was taking excellent care of the premises, and it couldn't be Dale, who hadn't even been here recently.

"This is absolutely lovely," Virtue said.

Dale shrugged. "Purp handles it."

"Who?"

"That's what I call him. Purp, because he's purple. He came with the house and knows what he's doing, so I kept him on." He glanced at her. "That's one of the benefits of being good instead of evil. Instead of killing competent folk, I use them. In fact I have received more material things from doing good than I ever did doing evil. If my evil self had known that, he might have changed on his own, not needing your bite." He was teasing her.

She sighed. "To think I wasted good saliva." She was teasing him back.

Benny stayed out of it. Dale had destroyed her coven and marked her for rape and death, yet she had forgiven him and treated him as a friend. She had bitten him to suppress his dark side and transform him to the good person he was now. In her position, Benny doubted he could have been so generous. But she was Virtue; there was no other woman like her. He loved her and would gladly die for her. He hated this horrible illness that had come upon her.

They came to the front veranda, where a remarkable man greeted Dale warmly. He was dressed in ornate blue livery, and was of average stature. But that was where his conventionality ended. His skin was red with light purple polka dots, and his hair was red and purple striped. His eyes were indefinite, appearing to Benny like marble in moonlight, with a subdued glow. Had he met this man in a dark alley he would have been concerned for his life; there was an aura of danger about him. This had to be Purp.

Dale introduced them. "This is Purp, my head butler. Without him, this house would be a wreck." Benny saw the man wince slightly at the term "house." Dale didn't mean to insult it; he simply had a lower brow vocabulary.

"And these are my friends Benny and his wife Virtue," Dale said. "She's a vamp, but she's the best person I know, and will be treated accordingly."

Benny saw Purp's trace reactions to that, too. Evidently he was annoyed that Dale had brought friends, which meant more work for the household staff, and that one of them was a vampire. Prejudice against vampires was widespread. But the word had been given: these were honored guests. The butler would obey.

Beside Benny, Virtue froze. She did not like Purp. Not at all.

"Understood," Purp said smoothly. "However, there is one other thing."

"Spit it out."

"There is an Amazon."

"You booted her out, of course," Dale said.

Purp almost smiled. "One does not exactly boot an Amazon. Not if one values one's health. One is polite and does not touch one's weapon. She insists on talking with you."

"Oh, sh--" Dale glanced at Virtue. "ucks. Then I'll deal with her. I'll d--" He paused again, momentarily. "arn well touch *my* weapon. Bring her up."

Benny saw Virtue form the trace of a smile. Dale was making a show of avoiding his normal course language in her presence because of Purp, though when they were alone he didn't bother. They were friends who could share more than language without offense. It was part of his statement about her guest status. No one mistreated a declared friend of Dale's, in or out of his mansion. Not even himself.

"I will speak for myself." A tall woman strode from the shadow of the veranda. She wore a loose red tunic that covered her left shoulder and breast and dropped to her knees. A double bladed sword hung from a strap cinching her taut midriff. Her exposed body was decorated with tattoos, piercings, and other tribal markings. Her blond hair was bound in a dozen tight dreadlocks that surrounded her neck. "Helena Amazon. I know who the three of you are; I overheard the introductions. May I make my case?"

Benny noticed that the Amazon's exposed right breast was marvelously formed, full yet erect; absolutely no sag there. Tattoos circled it, and there was a small silver ring through the nipple.

Virtue's finger snapped against his thigh warningly. She had no fear of competition, but did not want him to embarrass himself by too obvious an inspection. He had indeed been in danger of doing that.

"Make it and begone," Dale said tightly. His hand, as promised, was on the hilt of his sword, a plain challenge to the Amazon.

Helena smiled thinly, not at all fazed. "Perhaps we shall meet in the competition." She seemed to be quite ready for that. "But at the moment I have a problem. The tournament has summoned warriors from afar, I among them, and the local facilities are full. I am sure there are men who would gladly share, but I do not care to meet their price. So I come to ask the favor of a room of your fine mansion. I will pay."

Dale's demeanor changed. "Make truce, and you can share my room and bed."

"I mean to win a prize and marry the Emperor's son, so I must remain chaste for that. I proffer this instead." She held up a bright gold coin.

"Damn," Dale said, not editing his language for this recipient, which was another indication of contempt. "They say there's no lusty fun for a man like an Amazon, when she has a mind to. But I know what you mean. I had better stay celibate myself for the duration if I mean to marry the Emperor's daughter. Make truce, be my guest, friend status, warrior's code; we have a common objective."

"Truce. Friend status. Accepted. I'm glad you understand." Helena extended her empty hand.

Dale took it and formally shook it. They did understand each other.

"I will show you the residence," Purp said with resignation.

It turned out to be a fair miniature tour. The front door was made of pure pearl, surely more costly by itself than the whole house of an ordinary citizen. Inside was an indoor mock forest of cedar trees. It appeared to be snowing in the room, but the temperature was comfortable. There was even a little village of gnomes living in the forest. Benny tried not to smile, because they looked like typical lawn gnomes, with little red hats and different colored clothing and small beards.

"Are they real?" Benny asked, suspecting that the whole thing was illusion.

"Oh, yes," Dale said. "I let them move in after their original village was attacked by wolves."

Purp's jaw tightened. Evidently this had not been his preference.

They passed through the forest and entered the main house. The great room seemed to have walls made of pearl, with roses of different colors growing inside, not on, the walls themselves. It was both a parlor and a library.

"Lovely," Virtue murmured.

All the rooms were ornately decorated. The Amazon was given one with a pitched battle motif, and Benny and Virtue had one with the walls covered in a fresco of gnomes similar to the Fox Den.

"I had the room painted for you in case you ever visited," Dale explained.

"Thank you," Virtue said. "We do feel more at home here."

Apart from that, they were ensconced in a delightful suite with a view of the central courtyard, where a fountain played. But Virtue had no further strength for appreciation. She used the sanitary facility, stripped off her outer clothing, and collapsed on the plush bed.

She was not being seductive. It was the blood malady. "Oh, Virtue!" Benny breathed, sitting beside her. "I wish I could help you."

"Just keep that snide butler and that warrior woman away from me." Then she smiled faintly. "I read their minds. Dale still wants to get into her armored pants for a night's reveling without respect. She knows it and is annoyed. They're under a hospitality truce that neither much likes, but they will honor it to the letter. There'll be no panky."

"That's amusing," Benny agreed.

"Don't you have something to do, like practicing for the tournament or ogling that Amazon? Let me sleep in peace."

"But, Virtue, how can I leave you when you're in pain?"

She touched his hand. "I know you mean well, Benny. But my pain is worse when your mind is amplifying it. Please, get away from me. I am perfectly safe here."

"Oh." He stood and withdrew.

He went to the courtyard. There Dale and Helena were facing off. She was all the way naked now, and startlingly beautiful despite the body art. Benny remembered that Amazons preferred to fight nude, so that clothing would not inhibit their moves.

"Ah, there you are, Benny," Dale called. "We were waiting for you. We need a referee to call the scores."

"You expected me?" Benny asked, surprised.

"We knew Virtue needed her rest, and she couldn't get it with you hovering over her."

Oh, Benny thought. Sometimes it seemed that he was the last to catch on to a situation. So he changed the subject. "You can't fight," Benny protested. "You're under truce."

"We're not fighting, we're practicing, so as to be in fit shape for the tournament. Hel's earning her keep this way."

Hel? Was he already that familiar with her? "It looks from here as if you're flirting with each other. She's giving you a fantastic eyeful."

"That, too," Dale agreed with good humor, and Helena smiled. Their mutual hostility seemed to be abating.

Now Benny saw that they were flourishing padded wooden swords. They were serious about both the practice and the truce.

They went at it with vigor, thrusting and parrying. Dale deflected Helena's thrust, then smacked her bare bottom with the flat of his sword.

"Score, Dale," Benny announced, stifling a grin.

"Don't you wish that was your hand," Helena teased him.

"Oh, yes." They were fencing with words as well as swords.

They fought again, battling each other with renewed vigor. Helena whirled, causing her hair and breasts to swing out in a way that popped Benny's eyes. But as she completed her turn, her sword was out of place and Dale got another opportunity. He went to smack her bottom—and suddenly the flat of her sword knocked his wrist, almost disarming him. He could have lost his hand, with a real sword.

"Score Helena," Benny said. So the Amazon had let him score the first time, to set him up for the second. Benny should have caught that ploy, but that fabulous body distracted him.

"You certainly know how to use your weapons," Dale said.

"Did you think we fight bare just to keep our motions free?"

"A man could really lose his head," Dale agreed wryly. "Some do."

They continued, appearing evenly matched. Then Purp

showed up. "The cook wants your preference for dinner. She doesn't know the new guests."

"Any kind of meat, as long as it's raw," Helena said.

"Damn," Dale said. "Take over here, Benny. I've got to go straighten that cook out."

"But--"

"Take your turn," Helena said as Dale handed him the wooden sword and walked away.

So Benny faced the bare Amazon. It was quickly evident that he was no match for her. She smacked his rear repeatedly, while he made nary a score.

"You have to stop looking at my body and focus on your technique," Helena said.

"I know it," he agreed ruefully.

"You're not much, but you have magic. I can feel it. You're dangerous."

"You can tell that just by looking at me?"

"It's more of an aura. We Amazons know how to assess our opponents."

They resumed, but the mismatch was so evident that it seemed pointless to continue.

"Dally a while," Helena said as she washed off her sweaty body in the outdoor shower, then shook herself dry. That popped his eyes again.

"Why? You surely have better things to do than spend more time with me."

"It's the mystery. I've been trying to fathom your magic, but it eludes me. That aggravates me. Do you care to trade favors? All I want is to know its nature. I swear not to tell anyone else."

"I'm married. Anyway, you're supposed to be pristine."

She laughed as she donned her tunic. She wore nothing

under it, unless her black sandals counted. "You men have single track minds. That severely limits you. Favors can be of any kind."

Oh, Benny thought. "My wife doesn't like you."

"Of course she doesn't, and I don't like her. This is not personal. It's not even sexual; she has no jealousy of me in that respect. It has to do with the history of vampires and Amazons."

"She—she's ill. I want her to know she has nothing to fear from you."

"You want me to be her friend? That would be difficult."

"No. Merely to help safeguard her. She—she doesn't like Purp either."

"Now that's interesting. *I* don't like Purp."

"Well, he tried to keep you out of the mansion."

"That was his duty. I don't fault him for that. This is something else. There's a mystery about him, too, and it's a sinister one. But I trust him to do his duty to Dale, and he is not a present danger. I don't have to like him."

"That's the favor I want. For you to help my wife if she needs it."

"Done. Tell her that. Now tell me."

"My magic manifests only when I'm in deadly danger. I discorporate. That is, I become a ghost for a moment. If someone wrapped me in chains and threw me in the sea, I would ghost my way out of them and swim to the surface. But I try to stay out of any situation where I might need it, so it hardly seems to exist. I prefer that it not be known, as that would weaken its protection."

She nodded. "That makes sense. It matches my impression. If you were about to be killed in a fight, that would save you. Thank you."

Benny shrugged. "It's just the exchange of favors."

"Yes. I will honor it. Your wife will understand."

They returned to their rooms. Virtue was awake and evidently feeling better; the rest had helped. Her malady did tend to come and go.

"I—I hope I did the right thing," Benny said.

She read his mind. "You nullified the Amazon!"

"I didn't want you to have to fear her. You have more than enough trouble already. She says the mischief is not personal, but between your species. She—she seems like a decent sort. And she doesn't like Purp."

Virtue laughed. "That will have to do. I will not treat her like an enemy."

"I think we need all the friends we can get in a strange country like this."

She did not comment further. "Time to get ready for dinner."

"Time," he agreed, relieved that she wasn't angry with him for making the deal with the Amazon.

The copious closets had an array of clothing that fit them. How could Dale have known their sizes so accurately? "It's incidental magic," Virtue said as she donned a pale pink evening dress. "I can feel its shaping. This will fit any woman, and your suit will fit any man."

"I didn't know Dale had magic like that."

"I doubt he does. That purple butler surely handles such details."

"Yet you don't like Purp."

"He's obviously highly competent at his job. It's his heart I don't trust. I can't read his mind. Why does he hide it?"

"Butlers must see many private things they aren't

supposed to give away."

"You're so trusting. That's part of what I love about you." She kissed him, and then checked herself in the mirror. It was not true that vampires did not reflect; she was stunningly lovely in the form-fitting dress. Her hair coursed like a pale river to her knees.

"Oh, Virtue!" Benny breathed. "You are so much more than your body, but your body is matchless."

"You haven't seen the Amazon in a formal yet."

He laughed, embarrassed. How could any dress improve on Helena naked?

"Exactly."

That didn't help.

Dinner was a banquet with so many exotic entries that Benny could not identify or even count them. Benny reached to fill his glass, but Virtue stayed his hand. That was all the warning he needed; he found another pitcher.

Helena was seated across the table from them, wearing a kind of skullcap. She caught Virtue's eye. "We must talk," she said tersely. "After dinner, privately." Virtue nodded.

In due course dessert was served, in the form of a cake in the shape of a peacock with his tail spread wide. The servers cut pieces from it for each guest.

Then music started. Benny couldn't see any orchestra; it seemed to come from the walls.

Dale stood up from his place at the head table, and the servers quickly slid it away and out of the room. He crossed to their table and stood by Helena. "Will you do me the honor of the first dance?"

The Amazon stood. Now Benny saw her outfit, which had been concealed by the table and a napkin. It was startlingly apt, metallic blue that covered her breasts but displayed her figure to perfection. She drew off the skullcap and let her hair tumble down around her shoulders in soft waves, like a field of wheat in a breeze. The dreadlocks were completely gone. She was so beautiful that Benny froze in place, staring, until Virtue unobtrusively nudged him.

"I will," Helena agreed, and took his hand.

Benny and Virtue stood, and the table slid away. Now the center of the room was clear.

Dale and Helena danced, and Benny was amazed again. They were exquisite, a perfect couple, their steps exactly matching both the music and each other. He knew they could fight, but this was a completely different venue.

Virtue took his hand. "I will guide you," she murmured, and he felt her presence in his mind. Then they danced with similar finesse, and Virtue was as spellbinding as Helena, albeit in a gentler mode.

Then, an instant or an hour later, they were back in their room. There was a knock on the door. They expected Helena, but it was Dale. "May we talk?"

"Sure," Benny said, surprised as they took seats. "I thought you'd be with the Amazon."

"She elected to retire, suddenly. I fear I may have angered her, which was the last thing I wanted to do." He looked at Virtue. "I thought you might have an insight."

Virtue shook her head. "I can't read minds well in public. There are too many, and their traces tend to overlap, so it's like a mass of interlocking spaghetti. I am not good with Amazons anyway; they tend to be hostile to vampires in more than one manner. But I will say that you looked like the perfect couple."

"I thought we were. I wasn't going to try to despoil her for the tournament; I just wanted to talk with her, to get to know her better. I've never encountered an Amazon socially before." He took a deep breath. "I think I love her."

Just like that? Yet Benny had fallen for Virtue as rapidly. "But what of Nadia?" he asked.

"There is another part of the framework. I lied about our situation; we are separated. Her current interest is in a younger, more handsome man. I was too embarrassed to admit it publicly."

"That must be why she's away from the inn," Virtue said. "She knew I'd read her mind if she got close to me."

"Yes, I think so," Dale agreed. "So now I am free to seek another woman. I thought a princess would be fine, if I won her. But now, suddenly, today, all I can think of is Helena. And she seems not to want to talk with me. I don't know what to make of it." He sighed. "I thought maybe you, Virtue, being another woman, could tell me."

Virtue shook her head. "I think for that you need another Amazon. I am not party to their thought processes."

"Still, you may help. Since you bit me and suppressed my evil side—and I don't fault you for that, I bless you—I seem to have lost a lot of memory from the events of my life after I killed the orphans at Alsbury. It might be some divine act of mercy, since the new-found guilt of my actions might lead me to suicide. You—the two of you—knew me then, so you might have some insight. Could there be something from there that Helena knows about and remembered? I know I did a monstrous amount of evil."

Virtue was uncertain. "I am sure there are folk who will never forgive you. But I did not hear of you interacting much with Amazons, and in any event they are a hard-nosed lot, cynical to the point of cruelty. Helena would have understood your evil side better than most, and not entirely disagreed with it. In any event, if she carried a grudge from there, she would have let you know upfront, and challenged you to a duel of honor. She did not."

"Instead she danced with me," Dale said wonderingly. Then he got an alarming notion. "Could she have been vamping me—no offense—to garner my interest, before coldly shutting me down?"

Virtue shook her head again. "As I said, I really don't understand Amazons. But all that I do know of them is that they are not much for social subtlety. If she wanted to hurt you, she would do it with her sword, not her beauty." Her mouth quirked. "She would use her body to distract you to make you vulnerable to her sword, not to win your heart."

"Yet it is her beauty that is doing it," Dale said. "When I first saw her, I wanted to get her for a night in bed, and move on in the morning. But now I'd rather marry her."

Virtue spread her hands, as perplexed as he.

Benny brought out the twin-barreled pipe that Cycleze had given him. "I wonder if this would help? It offers peace and insight when correctly smoked."

"I remember that pipe," Dale said. "It is very special. It provides mental purity. Cycleze used charms like that a lot. He was one of the most powerful beings I ever knew."

Benny laughed. "You defeated Cycleze in combat when the two of you fell out. In fact you killed him."

"Maybe. My memory is foggy there, too. But if I had not made it to the Monastery of the Protector, I would have died from my injuries from that fight. He transformed into a chimera and nearly ripped me in half...you saw the scars from his teeth. The only way I defeated him was by going berserk. Even then I barely survived." He stood. "I think I have intruded more than enough. I apologize again for what

I did to your mouth." He departed before Benny could try to reassure him on that score.

"So we don't know what's with the Amazon," Virtue said. "I thought she would come to see me."

"Maybe tomorrow," Benny said. He looked at her. "Virtue, you are so beautiful tonight. Would--"

She cut him off with a kiss and led him to the bed. She was well familiar with his passion, and always obliged it.

In the morning they woke to a knock on the door. It was a servant delivering breakfast on a cart. "Room service," the maid explained.

Benny and Virtue exchanged a look. They had never heard of this. But of course they were unaccustomed to upper class life.

"When you are through," the maid said, "just push the cart out into the hall. It will find its way back to the kitchen."

"Uh, thank you," Benny said faintly.

Soon they met Dale in the great room. "The Imperial City is on the top of a mountain," Dale said. "The only way to actually get there is by air ship. There's a ferry from the local village."

"Then we'd better catch it," Benny said.

"No need. The estate includes such a ship. Purp will sail it."

Virtue glanced around. "Where is Helena?"

"It seems she departed before dawn, on her own." Dale grimaced. "I must really have teed her off."

And the Amazon had not even stayed to talk with Virtue, after arranging it. That was curious indeed.

"Maybe she intends to return," Benny suggested. "After fetching something she urgently needed."

"No," Dale said firmly.

"Why not?"

"Because she left the gold coin in her room, on the carefully made bed," Dale said grimly. "She paid for her keep in money. She's gone."

"Oh, that's too bad," Virtue said, wincing.

"Bad?" Benny asked. "What's wrong with it?"

"It's a deadly insult," Virtue said. "It means she bought his hospitality rather than accept it as a friend. It means she's not his friend."

"And I am insulted," Dale said. "I love her, but I hate her."

"Why the conflict?" Benny asked, still not quite getting it. "Why not just dismiss her as a prospect that didn't work out, and go after the Emperor's daughter?"

"That is not easy," Virtue said. "Helena is good looking, she's a warrior, and she honors the warrior code. She is very much his type of woman. When she accepted his hospitality, and even danced with him, she signaled her amenability to courtship, knowing his interest. Then, once she had the hook in, she dashed it, knowing he could not simply dismiss her. That's deadly. It bespeaks malice aforethought."

Benny remained confused. He had not gotten any impression of malice from the Amazon; she had seemed like a fair-minded person. "But—but couldn't something have come up unexpectedly, so she had to depart immediately? So she left the coin to show she didn't mean to cheat him, and left?"

"No," Virtue said. "She could have explained to Dale or a servant on the way out. Instead she lacked the courtesy even to tell him why. She threw his generosity in his face. That compounds the insult."

And Dale did not question her analysis. This was bad

indeed.

"We must get moving," Dale said.

And what would happen when Dale encountered Helena in the tournament?

Chapter 10

The air ship was a huge cylindrical balloon with a tiny gondola below. But when they boarded the gondola it turned out to be a full house in itself, complete with family room, kitchen, bathroom, and bedrooms. Purp, piloting it, was not to be seen; it seemed the cockpit was separate.

Benny and Virtue gazed out the round windows, thrilled to see the landscape below. The field of vision expanded as the craft floated upward, showing fields, forest, ponds, and the local village.

Then they approached a single high mountain with a flattened top, as if a giant had cut it off with a monstrous knife; a mesa. The mountain slopes were steep cliffs bare of vegetation; indeed, there was no access here, unless there was a spiraling tunnel within the mountain itself.

On that top was a walled city. "Why do they need a wall?" Virtue asked. "Nobody is going to raid from outside unless they come by air, and then they would float over the wall."

"To stop folk from accidentally stepping off the edge during a thick fog," Dale explained.

"Where do they get their water?" Benny asked.

"They have a deep central well. Very deep. Mostly they harvest water from the frequent fogs. They have some very nice gardens, completely without weeds or invasive species."

The air ship glided down outside the wall, in fact just off the edge of the plain. There was a huge gate set below the top surface. The ship hovered while signals passed between it and the proprietors of the gate. Then the gate slid open and the ship entered what turned out to be the largest tunnel Benny had ever seen or imagined. Odd unflickering torches lined its circular wall, showing the route.

The gate slid closed behind them. There would be no invasion by this access either. This mountain was secure.

They docked and were tied in place. Guards intercepted them as they emerged from the gondola, demanding information. Purp started to speak, but they rudely brushed him aside.

"Stay with the ship," Dale told him. "They won't bother you there. I will get you a pass, in due course."

Purp nodded and returned to the ship. Benny couldn't blame him for being annoyed.

Dale showed his identification and vouched for Benny and Virtue. Then each had to dip his or her left hand into a pot of blue dye. It didn't hurt, but it marked them quite plainly as visitors, not residents. "It'll wear off in a week or so," Dale said. "But by then we should be done here."

They climbed a narrow stairway to the surface. Immediately it was clear that the Imperial City was huge and lovely, a virtual garden paradise. They saw citizens going about their routine business, garbed beautifully, male and female. They cast dark glares at the visitors.

"They don't even know us," Benny said, nettled.

"They hate all blue hands," Dale said. "Ignore them."

"Smells like bigotry to me."

"They have their reasons."

The coliseum where the tournament would be was a huge round edifice with its own guarded entrance. Dale identified himself again, and they were admitted. They were required to park their weapons and take special magical non-lethal weapons akin to wooden swords but more sophisticated, as these would signal the referees whether any given strike was to be considered incidental or lethal.

Now they were divided into groups for combat. Virtue, as a noncombatant, was given a seat in the amphitheater; Benny and Dale were given opponents.

Benny pondered again just why he was here. He had no need to compete, and was by no means a top warrior. Yet somehow he had gone along. Now, suddenly, he knew why: if he won the keg of gold and jewels, he could use the money to purchase the best possible treatment for Virtue's ailment. That was more than reason enough.

His first opponent was a frost giant: a big blue-skinned man with an ax. His blue left hand hardly showed against his skin. He looked dangerous, but Benny reminded himself that this was a non-lethal tournament whose weapons were magically enchanted to deliver signals, not wounds. There was no actual danger here, other than the humiliation of getting trounced. Which was probably Benny's early destiny. But Virtue was watching, and other members of a vast audience, and he had to make a bold show of it.

Actually an ax was not considered to be comparable to a sword. All the target had to do was avoid the swing, and counter with an inside stroke to finish it. Even Benny could do that much.

The referee stood impassively. He would not intervene

unless there was a breach in protocol. Each ring had its own referee.

The combatants strode toward each other. Benny raised his sword to a guard position, ready to try for a good technique. But the frost giant lacked any subtlety at all. He simply charged in, swinging his ax with horrible velocity right at Benny's head. He had no time to parry or duck; the blade swept in to chop his head in half.

Then the giant was stumbling, unbalanced. Benny whirled and swung his sword, aiming for the neck, in an automatic reflex. He got it.

A klaxon sounded. Benny had scored! In fact he had figuratively beheaded the frost giant, abruptly winning the match.

Belatedly he realized that his talent had manifested. The threat had not been real, but it seemed that his magic was not sophisticated enough to distinguish reality from appearance. When the ax seemed about to chop half his head off, he had ghosted momentarily. It had passed through him, and the giant had lost his balance, expecting solid contact. That had made him vulnerable, and Benny had taken advantage of it without thinking. So he was a first round winner, to his surprise. He glanced at the referee, but there was no reaction; it seemed magic was permitted as long as it was not lethal.

Virtue caught his eye and nodded. He truly had won.

Meanwhile he saw that Dale had fought in another ring, against an elf. Elves were small and slender, but they knew how to fight, and Dale had had to be careful because any small error could lead to his undoing. His care paid off, and he defeated the elf, winning the round.

Helena was in a third ring, naked except for her tattoos, handily dispatching an ogre. There were two other rings, with other competitors.

Then the second round came. Benny faced a swamp troll, a vaguely manlike figure covered in fungus. Its left hand was blue and it wielded a clumsy-looking club. But Benny knew that was deceptive; the clubs of swamp trolls were not used for concussive force so much as for messing up the weapons and perceptions of opponents. He would try to avoid contact with it.

But the troll gave him no choice. It came at him swinging that club. Benny backed away, parrying with his sword, and muddy chips flaked from the club. They dropped to the floor, where they bounced like little balls. One struck the cuff of the referee's trouser-leg, and the material burst into flame. Just so.

The troll swung again, and Benny blocked it again. But this time the blade of his sword sank into the club and stuck there. He yanked, but it did not come free. It was trying to disarm him!

The troll hauled his club back, and Benny was drawn with it, unable to let go lest he lose his weapon. He was being lifted into the air! So he jumped higher, and clubbed the troll in the face with both feet. The troll went down, and Benny landed beyond, sword still stuck.

He spun around, put a foot on the troll's arm, and yanked on his sword with both hands. The club did not let go, but the troll did; now the club was held by the sword. The troll scrambled up again and charged. Benny heaved the sword around, and the stuck club bashed the troll. It fell, unconscious, knocked out, ironically, by its own weapon.

The klaxon sounded. Benny had won, again. He knew it was more by luck than skill, but often it was that way in battle. He stood on the club and hauled on his sword with both hands, finally freeing it.

Meanwhile Dale fought a dwarf. Again, size was no indication of skill; some dwarfs were deadly. This one had a stout club which he swung viciously at Dale's legs. Dale, used to larger foes, had difficulty orienting on the quickly moving low figure. He had to keep jumping to avoid the blows, as parrying them was awkward. Finally he did it the inelegant way: he bashed straight down with his club, striking at the dwarf's head. The dwarf dodged, but Dale swung again, and again, repeatedly, very fast, like hammering in a spike, and finally scored, winning the match. "Good game!" the dwarf said with no ill favor. He was of course unhurt.

Helena fought a tiger-like creature that used no weapon, only its teeth and claws, but was fast and powerful. The claws glistened, suggesting poison that might stun her if a drop struck her flesh, and of course all of her flesh was exposed. But she had evidently encountered such creatures before. She dodged around it and cut off its swishing tail. The klaxon sounded; it seemed that was a lethal blow. She had known.

Benny's third opponent was someone he recognized: Red Rat Flack, whom he had seen at the Fox Den before this excursion, and who had hired the goon who had mistaken him for Dale. He had never liked the man, and not just because of the savage stories about him; he knew from firsthand experience that the man was deviously dangerous. Mainly, it was that Flack had poisoned Virtue, his blood being hostile to vampires, so that she now suffered worsening sieges of illness. But Benny had no choice: he had to fight him, or default.

"I remember you, farm boy," Flack sneered as he unlimbered his two large scimitars. "Took up with a vampire whore, didn't you? I fixed that slut real good, didn't I? Gave her a taste of her own foul medicine. After I dispatch you, bumpkin, maybe I'll take her, so she'll know what a real man feels like."

But this, at least, Benny was wise to. The man was trying to taunt him into losing his temper and acting foolishly. That suggested that he wasn't sure of victory by honest means. Did he know about Benny's magic? Probably not, so that was a secret weapon. "Why don't you close your potty mouth and try to act like a warrior, rat face?" Benny asked. "You scared to take me on? That's why you're stalling?"

It worked. If there was one thing such bullies hated, it was getting teased back in kind. Flack charged him, swinging the scimitars in a scissors motion calculated to cut Benny in half. Benny jumped high, letting them cross harmlessly beneath him, then landed on the man's arms, pinning them down, while poking his sword in his face. It was a surprise move that caught the man off-guard, and it was effective; the klaxon sounded, signaling his victory.

Flack swore villainously and shot a dagger out of his gauntlet to stab Benny. It was an illegal weapon, and it cut him in the midriff.

"Foul!" the referee cried, and signaled the guards. But Flack, enraged, was undeterred. A second dagger appeared in his hand, and he had time to use it before the guards got there.

Then a bolt of lightning shot out and struck Flack, sending him across the ring. What had happened?

Dale laughed as the guards pounced on Flack. "I was saving that for the tournament. It's a new trick I learned recently: the mage cry that sends lightning rather than sound. I thought it might be needed sooner."

So it seemed. Why hadn't Benny's magic worked to spare him the stab wound?

The tournament was suspended while the guards hustled Flack out of the arena. The head of the guards returned to report to them. "That man is hereby banned from the tournament, by order of the Emperor," he said grimly. "He used an unsanctioned weapon, a dagger charmed against magic."

Suddenly Benny knew why that dagger had scored on him: it was enchanted to resist his magic. That was worth knowing—that he was not proof against such weapons.

The tournament resumed. Benny's matches had been concluded quickly, so now he could relax with Virtue. They watched Dale's third match. It was against a Sorai, a winged human. Benny could tell immediately that the man was highly competent, and he was not bound to the ground; he leaped high, spread his wings, and circled Dale before landing and attacking. Dale was not fazed; he turned in place to face the man, and parried accurately.

This match was not concluded quickly. The two traded strike for strike, neither finding opportunity to score. The other matches finished, and the audience focused on this one, fascinated by the skillful interplay. They were evenly matched at the highest level of skill.

Then Dale shifted into berserker mode. This was evidently new to the Sorai; he retreated, fighting well, but was unable to withstand the sheer ferocity of the attack. He leaped high, spread his wings, and struck down from above in a nice maneuver, but Dale was ready for it. He leaped high himself, and struck the other man's sword with such power that it flew from his hand, disarming him.

No klaxon sounded. Disarmament was not the same

as a lethal strike.

The man landed, closing his wings, and raised his fists. This was disaster against a sword, but he refused to quit. He had the courage of a true warrior.

Dale dropped his own sword and tackled the Sorai and there was a murmur of appreciation from the audience for the sportsmanship. They boxed, and clinched. The Sorai spread his wings and lifted them both in the air, but Dale would not let go. He hung on to one of the man's arms while striking his torso with his other fist. The Sorai, higher in the air, struck at Dale's head. All the blows hurt, at least were scored as hurting; Benny could see that.

Finally Dale wrenched his body upward and scored on the man's head with his feet. It was a remarkably athletic maneuver. Now at last the klaxon sounded; that was a definitive blow.

They landed, and separated, each marked with color where blows had landed. They bowed to each other as the audience broke into applause.

"That was one of the greatest bouts in history," the head referee said, awed.

"I like that man," Dale said as tournament maidens addressed his apparent injuries and those of his opponent, cleaning off the colors. Had it been real combat, both would have been near unconsciousness.

The matches were done, the five winners determined. They were Dale, Benny, Helena, a desert giant, and a frost dwarf with pure white skin and hair. "The Emperor will meet with you tomorrow," the head referee said. "Each winner will receive a prize of his or her choice."

"But I'm not a great warrior," Benny protested as they walked out of the arena. "I don't belong in that elite group.

The Sorai is far better than I am."

"It's the luck of the draw," Dale said. "I agree he is most worthy, and I would like to fight by his side, but he was in the wrong competitor group. Life is not always fair."

Benny knew that it was so, but he still didn't like it.

Meanwhile Helena approached Virtue. "We must talk before I go," she said.

"I am feeling a little faint," Virtue said. "Perhaps another time."

"There may not be another time."

Virtue opened her mouth to speak, but paused in place. Then she started to fall. The Amazon leaped forward to catch her. Still she sagged; she was unconscious, victim of a sudden siege. They were definitely getting worse. Benny had not been close enough to catch her.

Helena picked her up and held her in her two strong arms. "I will take her where she needs to go. I know she is ill. That's what we need to talk about."

"Do it somewhere else," Dale gritted, wanting no part of the Amazon. Helena returned the favor, ignoring him.

The timing was awful, but Benny was the one who had asked Helena to relate to the vampire. He couldn't reverse himself now. "The air ship is best. Her things are there, and her bed is comfortable. In our chamber."

"Suit yourself." Dale stalked off.

Benny showed the way, and Helena carried Virtue. They entered the gondola, and the Amazon laid the vampire down on the bed.

Virtue woke. "I know your secret."

"And I know yours."

What were they talking about?

"I read your mind. You love him," Virtue said.

"And I felt your body. You are pregnant."

What? Benny thought.

Virtue glanced at him. "Sit down and stay out of this."

He sat down and was silent.

"I cannot ethically depart until I have done what I can for you," Helena said. "I made a deal with Benny, and I must honor it."

"Depart?" Virtue asked. "You have closed your mind; why should you go before receiving your prize?"

"Because I can't be near Dale. I have done him unforgivable injury, and we must never meet again."

"Ah, yes," Virtue agreed.

"But I have no personal quarrel with you, Virtue, and I know you are a good person. First a bit of background: the Amazons and the vampires go way back, historically, as you know, but you may not know enough. Over the centuries we have both helped and hindered each other. Vampires have bitten Amazons to give them berserker powers when they needed them, and Amazons have sent contingents to rout vampire enemies when that was required. But we have not always been friends, and some incidents have been ugly. You had good reason to be wary of me. This was not a thing I cared to explain to Benny, but I did trade favors with him and now I see the way to pay mine."

"There is no need," Virtue said. "I may not endure long enough to make much use of any favor anyway."

"There you are wrong," Helena said. "I know you suffered a reverse bite by the red rat, and are suffering the resulting illness. Amazons can also resist vampire bites, and even reverse them. The berserker effect was only when the Amazon accepted it. Some Amazons can even do the return blood poisoning, similar to what the red rat did to you. I repeat: you were wise to be wary of me. But there is one special effect I think you did not know about. When an Amazon with that power has a mind, she can counter other blood poisoning." She took a breath. "I am such an Amazon, and I have such a mind. I can cure you, Virtue. That is my favor to you, before I go. Bite me."

"Cure me?" Virtue breathed.

"Trust me. This will save you and your baby."

"But you have no call to do this much for me. All Benny gave you was a bit of information that you might have learned elsewhere anyway."

"And I have given you information. It is the right thing to do. Bite me." She proffered her bare shoulder. She smiled. "Make it a harmless bite."

Virtue did not argue further. She sat up, leaned over, and bit the Amazon.

"Oh!" That was Virtue, surprised.

"It takes a moment, but you will soon feel it spreading through your body. Rest and let it act. You will know within hours."

"I know already," Virtue said. "I feel the healing."

Benny was amazed. So it was working! Virtue would recover!

Helena stood. "My business here is done. Now I can depart. I am sorry we will never meet again."

Benny jumped to his feet. "The hell!"

Both Virtue and Helena looked at him, startled; they had evidently forgotten that he was present.

"But it is true, dear," Virtue said. "I am becoming cured, and our baby will be saved. You must believe me."

"I do believe you," Benny said. "But I am not going to let the Amazon simply walk out of here forever. She has given you far more than I gave her."

Helena's mouth twitched. "I will not lift a weapon against you in your wife's presence. But I doubt you can stop me."

"Virtue said you love Dale," Benny said. "That you have insulted him, and can't be forgiven. That's not true."

"Benny, this is complicated," Virtue said. "I have read her mind, and she is correct. The parameters of honor have a long history, and may not be abridged."

"Well spoken," Helena murmured.

But Benny would not let this pass. "Shut up, both of you, until I deal with this. I know about honor. So does Dale. This can be fixed." Then he turned and cupped his hands around his mouth. "Dale!" he called. "We need you here. Now."

The two women stared at each other, mutually appalled.

In moments Dale burst in, sword drawn. "What did she do?" he demanded.

"First a question," Benny said. "To what one person in the world do you owe the most?"

"Virtue," Dale said immediately. "She turned me from evil to good. It will take the rest of my life to repay her, if I can."

"Exactly. Is there anything in your power, in honor, she could ask of you that you would not do for her?"

"I would not rape her or kill her, even if she asked. Other than that, no."

Benny faced Virtue. "Ask him to forgive the Amazon. This he can honorably do, as he is the victim."

The jaws of both women dropped, and Dale looked stunned. Then Virtue rallied, catching on. "Dale, please forgive Helena."

The man's mouth worked for a moment before he got the reluctant words out. It was evident that he had been hit by what he least expected, and hardly knew how to cope with it. All he could do was accept it. "I forgive Helena."

The Amazon swung into action as if she had just seen an opening in a hard-fought battle, which was not far from the case. "Dale, I love you. I fled because I hated that I fell for you. It threatened to ruin everything. I had to alienate you so I could win and wed the Emperor's son and secure an excellent future for myself." She closed her eyes, wincing. "But then I realized that it was already too late. I don't care about the Emperor's son. All I want is to be with you."

Dale stared. "You rejected me because you loved me?"

"I did. It is the Amazon way. But now that you have so generously forgiven me, I will never reject you again. I love you. I mean that in the most passionate way." She kissed him as he stood bemused. "I will do my best to prove it in the next few minutes. Get me to a bed."

"Done!" he agreed, accepting this turn of events as readily as Helena had. He sheathed his sword, picked her up, she not resisting at all, and carried her out of the room.

"You're really getting better?" Benny asked Virtue, his uncertainty returning now that the tension had eased. "I wish--"

"I really am. I am not yet very far in my pregnancy, and my mind can feel their exploding passion. We should not be excluded. Get over here, lover, and do your manly duty."

Some duty! Benny charged her.

CHAPTER 11

After their romantic affair was done, Benny fell into a peaceful and deep sleep. This however, did not last. He opened his eyes to throaty laughter, like the sound of thousands of maniacal demons issuing from the bowels of the hell. It was dark, and in the distance was the familiar green light of the eye that stirred pure fear in Benny's heart. The cold tentacles were wrapped around his body, choking the life from him. "This can't be happening!" Benny said to himself.

"Oh, but it is, stupid boy!" the voice spoke.

Benny was speechless. He closed his eyes and did his best to summon his ghost-magic just long enough to escape the life-crushing vice of the tentacles, but it was no use. Benny's magic was nonexistent.

"You are weak, aren't you boy?" More laughter pierced the air.

"Who the hell are you?!" Benny screamed.

The laughter stopped abruptly. "Isn't it obvious, waif? I am the Grand Exalted Cyclops! The age of the Kudgel has come, and nothing will stand in our way!"

The eyeball burned through Benny's eyes, and he

screamed in agony. It felt like his brain was going to explode inside his head and his body seized with convulsions.

"Wake up!" Virtue's voice ricocheted inside Benny's head.

He shot up, drenched in sweat yet cold as an icicle. He saw Virtue's worried look, and behind her three other people: Dale, Helena and Purp. All were worried except for Purp, who had a bemused grin on his face.

"Good grief, kid. Your vampire wife must've given it to you good last night." Purp said.

"None of your sarcasm," Dale told the man before redirecting to Benny. "You were suffering convulsions and screaming something about a Cyclops. What happened?"

Benny looked at Virtue, who nodded and addressed Dale's question, "Before you and Bum arrived at the Fox Den, Benny was suffering from terrible nightmares about an evil force trying to kill him. I still can't see into the dream, but I can read Benny's memory. It was the leader of the Kudgels…the Cyclops."

Dale and Helena looked at each other with worried looks. Purp rolled his eyes and stepped forward.

"Oh, enough of that nonsense! The Kudgels don't have a leader. The Grand Exalted Cyclops is just an old myth. Anyone with a formal education will know that." Purp looked at them all and then shrugged. "But then again, considering the lot I'm talking to…"

Benny knew that Purp was using subtle sarcasm, trying to hint at the uneducated superstition the butler thought the whole affair to be.

"Well, it is certainly trying to scare Benny, whatever it is," Helena exclaimed.

"I'll admit I don't know what these dreams mean, as I am no seer like Virtue," Dale said, "but I know they can mean nothing good. And regardless of whether this Cyclops character is real, the Kudgels most certainly are."

Purp placed a hand on Dale's shoulder and rolled his eyes again. "Master, just because one breakaway thug holds some unknown grudge against you is no reason to suspect some grand conspiracy from that band of dumb brutes."

"I'll be all right, everyone. It was probably just the excitement from the tournament and last night." Benny didn't want to think about the dream any longer.

"Let's hope, for all of our sakes, that you're right," Dale said.

Purp sighed and rubbed his eyes with a gloved hand. "Well, if you warriors are done blabbing about your primitive superstitions, you should probably head for the imperial palace. It's almost noon and the feast will soon begin."

Purp turned and left the room, followed by Dale. Helena stayed while Virtue and Benny got dressed.

"That purple man is hiding something," Helena said, "I don't know what it is, but I don't like it."

"He ain't hiding anything. He's just a jerk," Benny said.

"No, Helena's right," Virtue said. "There's a lot more to that man than meets the eye. He has amazing control over his mind. His is the only mind that has ever been completely shut off to my telepathic abilities. Not a block like Helena's, walling me out when she chooses. It's more like peering into an empty void…not one thought. Not even a memory!"

Virtue finished putting on a formal yet practical outfit that Dale had brought for her. Helena was dressed in the same outfit and had the same dreaded hair as when Benny had first seen the female warrior.

"Um…don't you ladies want to wear something a little more formal? We are going to see the emperor of all Upper Sultry." Benny was busy trying to button a very fancy overcoat with what seemed to be hundreds of buttons.

"A guard told me that the victors were to wear whatever clothing we felt comfortable with," Helena said. "The Emperor apparently has no dress code for these kinds of events."

"Well in that case…."

Benny ripped off the monkey suit he had struggled to button. After throwing the rest of the outfit into the corner he selected a clean outfit similar to the one he wore for the tournament.

As they traversed the bustling streets of the Imperial City on their way to the palace, Benny took some time to take in his surroundings. The city was the largest and most beautiful he'd ever seen. He had been shocked at the size of Galver Dorn when he'd first visited it with Dale and Cycleze, but now that town seemed like a shanty. The buildings reached up into the sky and were of an exotic architecture he'd never seen before; gardens, manmade waterfalls, and sculptures filled the streets. Most of the citizens were extremely tall, like the border guard they had met outside the portal. These people all wore exotic clothing and seemed to shun Benny and his fellow travelers.

"These people are a bunch of snobs," Benny said to Dale.

"They're just cautious of foreigners, but I will admit it often impedes their judgments of others," Dale replied.

As they walked past an alley way, Benny saw a young

boy dressed in rags appear from the shadows. He was dirty and unkempt, but Benny could tell that he had green skin and yellowish hair. He mumbled something to Dale and held out his hands. The boy was a beggar. Dale, instead of driving off the boy as Benny thought he would, knelt down beside the kid and ruffled his hair. The kid smiled, revealing rotten teeth, and Dale handed him a gold coin. He jumped with glee and ran back into the shadows of the alley. The aristocrats gave cries of surprise and insult as he wound between their legs.

"He had green skin…" Helena said, "Is he of the same race as Purp?"

"You could say that…they are all human," Dale said. "They just have different colored skin. It's the side effect of the mass number of spells wizards used in the ancient civil wars between Upper and Lower Sultry. Some have red, purple or green skin, while others have striped, marbled or polka-dotted skin like Purp. They have a history of being abused and rejected because of their skin tones."

"But just because they have different colored skin doesn't make them any less important. If anything, I think it makes them all the more beautiful," Virtue said. She was clearly upset by the poor health of the green boy.

"I agree, but unfortunately racism is a disease that infests even a great nation like Upper Sultry. This is the main reason for Purp's bad attitude. His father was arrested and thrown in jail for stealing food for his starving family and his mother died of some sickness soon afterwards. They lived in the slums of this very city, and most of Purp's siblings died off…all save his sister." Dale stopped at the mention of his butler's relative.

"And where is his sister now?" Helena asked.

"She's a prostitute in the Imperial slums." Dale shed a tear when he said this. "Purp isn't a bad person. I know he comes off as a sarcastic prick sometimes, but he's had as hard a life as any could have….a lot harder than I ever had. I think I'm the first person to ever give Purp a place to call home. I respect him and he respects me."

Benny now understood a little better as to why he, Virtue and Helena all had such a bad feeling about the man. Purp was ashamed and hurt by his past, and put on a very cold, harsh attitude so he wouldn't be hurt again. He'd grown up without parents, watched his siblings starve, and his only surviving relative turned into a piece of meat for lusty nobles or worse. Benny looked at his female companions, whose facial features seemed to reciprocate his new-found understanding of the man they had misjudged.

"Why didn't you give his sister a place at your estate?" Benny asked Dale.

"I tried, Benny. The Protector knows I tried. But she refused." He wiped away another tear.

"But why would she refuse such an offer to have a clean home and even be with her brother? She'd rather live as a whore…as property for some horny aristocrat?" Helena clinched her fists, obviously annoyed by the mere thought.

"I guess when you have to live a certain way for so long, you don't know how else to act," Dale said.

They passed by the coliseum where the tournament had been held and followed a wide path to ornate gates made of what looked like pure gold. They passed through these into one of the largest courtyards Benny had ever seen. They walked a red carpet to the stairs of the great palace, where the Sorai Dale had fought stood smiling with his hand outstretched. He had curly golden hair and darkly tanned skin. The brilliance of the white feathers of his wings almost seemed whiter than the sun. He wore simple, but neatly cut trousers.

"I didn't get a chance to congratulate you for your victory in our bout yesterday." He smiled and rubbed a swollen bruise under his eye.

"Thank you, sir. If I didn't have the ability to enter berserk mode at will, I dare say you would have defeated me." Dale shook his hand.

"You're too modest, Dale."

"You know my name, but I don't know yours."

"Forgive me. You can call me Quill. My only regret is that I won't be able to meet the Emperor…I came a long way with the hopes of being in his presence, if even for a moment." Quill's face became wrinkled with a depressed frown.

Dale scratched his chin. "Come with us. Maybe there is a way you can get your wish after all."

They climbed the seemingly endless steps to another gate which appeared to be carved from black onyx. Two tall guardsmen with feather plumed helmets checked them before entering.

"I am Dale Beranger, and these are two of the other victors from the tournament, Benny Clout and Helena the Amazon." Dale pointed to his companions.

"Are these other two your desired guests?" one of the guards asked, pointing to Virtue and Quill.

"What do you mean?" Helena asked.

"Each victor is allowed to have one guest accompany them to the feast. Do you vouch for these two?" the guard asked.

"We must not have been paying attention…yes. Benny

will vouch for his wife, Virtue the Vampire. I will vouch for my new friend, Quill the Sorai," Dale said.

"Yes, I watched the bout between you two. The Emperor was most impressed. Enter and make yourself at home. You will be led to the dining hall when the time comes." The guards moved aside and pushed open the doors to the main entrance.

Chapter 12

The lounge where the warriors waited was even more lavishly decorated than Dale's palatial estate. The furniture was made from the finest woods and metals, and the tapestries were richly embroidered with coats of arms and scenes from the history of Upper Sultry. Aside from Benny, Dale and Helena, and their guests, the only other people waiting in the lounge were the other two tournament winners. One was a frost dwarf from the far north, beyond Upper Sultry. He had blood red eyes, snow white skin, hair and beard. He wore the fur of a snow leopard as his only piece of clothing, held at the waist by a belt. The battle hammer Benny had seen him with lay at his feet. He looked at Benny from his chair and nodded sternly. The other winner was a desert giant. He was almost 15 feet tall and had dark brown skin. He wore a turban on his head and had gold earrings. He wore a thick cloak that he kept wrapped tightly around him. Benny wondered if something was wrong with him, because through the cloak the giant's stomach seemed strangely distended. The doors on the far end of the hall opened and two more guards beckoned them to enter the dining hall.

"What are you going to choose for your reward?" Helena asked Benny.

"Well, I don't know. I was thinking about using the gold to buy a cure for Virtue, but since she's well now, I'll have to see. What about you two?" Benny smiled as Dale blushed.

"It would appear we have a similar problem…" Helena grinned and punched him hard on the shoulder.

"Just to meet the Emperor is a gift in and of itself," Quill said.

"I wonder what he's like," Virtue said.

They entered the dining hall, which was in the next room. There was a long table with what seemed like hundreds of chairs. They were designated to sit at the end closest to what they guessed was the Emperor's chair, since it was made of pure gold and larger than the rest. Benny sat between Virtue and the frost dwarf on one side, while Dale, Helena, Quill and the giant sat on the other side. Nearly twenty guards surrounded the table. Before Benny could gather in his surroundings, a small white hand shot up in Benny's face.

"Gulmang Du so crotak!" the dwarf mumbled.

"Huh?"

"It means hello, friend! My name is Kolpak. I saw your fight with the Red Rat…I'm glad he didn't succeed in killing you." Kolpak turned back to his plate of butter and rolls.

"Are you okay?" Benny asked.

Kolpak was sweating profusely and breathing hard, "I'm just not used to this heat."

Benny was perplexed, because he actually found the weather of Upper Sultry cold and soothing. But then again, if the dwarf was from the far northern mountains, then he would have spent almost his entire life in sub-zero temperatures. Benny then had an idea.

"My wife, here, is a vampire. She could give you a magic bite to help your body adjust to the warmer climate," Benny suggested.

"It would be an honor to assist a handsome dwarf knight such as you," Virtue chimed in.

The dwarf laughed and leaned back. "I appreciate the compliment but even I know I ain't handsome. Do your stuff, girly."

Virtue walked around to him, bent down, and lightly bit him on the neck. In an instant the dwarf stopped breathing hard and his countenance became more cheerful. "It's almost as if I'm back home in my cave!"

"That is just one of the perks of knowing a vampire." Benny winked at Kolpak.

Just then the sound of drumming filled Benny's ears and two normal sized humans dressed in red cloaks entered through the door behind the Emperor's seat. They blew a note and the doors behind them burst open. Light flooded into the room, causing the tournament winners to shield their eyes. At first Benny thought it was the sun blinding them, but then he realized the light emanated from a person.

"All rise for the Emperor of Upper Sultry! All hail the Son of the Sun!" a guard called.

The Emperor was over 10 feet tall and had long curly blond hair and beard. He was dressed in a bulky suit of golden battle armor with a sunburst mantle mounted to his armor, behind his head. Another sun was emblazoned across his breastplate, which had a face hammered into it. Light seemed to exude from his very skin. The only thing about his appearance that wasn't golden was the blood-red cape that trailed behind him. He smiled to the standing victors and bid them to sit back down, joining them at his seat. The smile on his face faded as he saw Dale.

"Mr. Beranger, remove your mask. We hide nothing here," he said.

Benny realized then that Dale had been wearing his prosthetic face since they had left Bluecorn Betty. Dale looked nervous at first, since Helena hadn't seen his real face. But after a reassuring nod from the Emperor, Dale slowly peeled off the face. Helena looked shocked at first, but then smiled.

"Dale, do me a favor and never wear that thing again. You have more character without it." Helena reached up and pulled the fake goatee off Dale's mouth and kissed him.

"Ah, how good it is to see true love." The Emperor smiled and looked around at the other guests. "It appears that Dale and Helena the Amazon are already well acquainted. Aside from them, our victors include Benny Clout from Gant, Kolpak from the northern mountains, and Toldnas the giant from the western deserts. We also have two visitors. Benny's wife, the lovely Virtue, and Quill the Sorai, whom I must compliment on his dual with Dale. It reminded me of the sparring sessions in my youth."

"Cut the crap! Where's my reward?" the giant Toldnas snapped.

Everyone was shocked by his rudeness, except for the Emperor, who simply smiled and held up his hand in a sign of benediction. "Soon, Toldnas. But first, enjoy the feast!"

The feast was by far the best Benny had ever had. It was a five course meal including many foods Benny had never seen before. It was topped off by a dessert consisting of a strange red fruit that had a spiky red rind and a mushy yellow interior that tasted like chocolate cake. Benny looked around the room. All of the guests seemed to enjoy the meal as much as he had, except for the giant, who seemed eager to get the meal over with. The Emperor lightly conversed with the group, and after the last person had finished the dessert, he stood up from his seat and began the formalities of dispensing the rewards from the tournament.

He raised his hand towards the door he had entered. "You all fought admirably, and for your victories I will now reveal the assorted prizes."

The doors opened and more guards poured out, escorting a handsome, well-dressed man about the Emperor's size, and a beautiful woman who stood about seven feet tall. These were the first two prizes, the chance to marry the son or daughter of the Emperor. Following them was a man holding a large scroll, which Benny assumed was the deed to a stately mansion in Upper Sultry. Then a group of large men carrying a huge chest entered the room, setting down the chest and opening it to reveal a heaping pile of gold and jewels. Several other prizes followed, including enchanted jewelry, fancy apparel and a suit of armor made of pure gold. The last thing to come in was an old man holding what looked like a common walking stick. However, when Benny stared at it he could tell that the piece of wood carried a very strong enchantment. This was something Benny could use. He had no need for a mansion. The Fox Den was the only home he ever needed or wanted. Fancy clothes and armor would only get one so far, and Benny doubted the quality of the items was of any real use to him. The stick, however, was a practical tool and could prove useful in the long run.

"So now that you see your options, you may chose,

beginning with Toldnas who was so eager to get the ball rolling." The Emperor chuckled and winked at Benny.

The giant walked up to the man holding the scroll and snatched it out of the guard's hands with two of his giant fingers.

"I choose the homestead!" Toldnas roared.

He returned to his seat, and Kolpak walked up to the chest of gold. "No disrespect to your highness, but I already have a mate and I've no desire for a second." Kolpak graciously kissed the princess' hand and walked over to place his hand on the chest of gold.

Dale and Helena stood together, the former addressing the Emperor, "Both Helena Amazon and I had originally come to the tournament in order to win the hands of your heirs. In the process, however, we have found a great passion for one another. This is a reward enough for both of us."

"So be it. These gifts are yours to accept or deny, there will be no ill will harbored towards you," the Emperor said.

"May you both live long, peaceful lives together," the prince said, bowing towards Dale and Helena.

Then the Emperor's gaze fell on Benny. "It looks like you are the last to choose a prize. You may accept my daughter's hand in marriage if you chose, however I doubt your wife, there, would approve."

Benny walked towards the old man holding the walking stick. "Your liege, I am not rich by any stretch of the imagination, nor do I feel that I deserve to stand in the same room as these great fighters behind me. My victories were of mere luck, especially in the case of Flack. I choose this stick, because of its practicality as a useful aid for my travels. Every adventurer needs a good staff to lean on sometimes, especially as I grow older. It will serve me well enough."

"It most certainly will." The Emperor sat back down and bid Benny to return to his seat. "Now we must discuss the other reasons why you are here."

The Emperor's attendants and children then left the room, leaving only the Emperor, his elite guard, and the warriors in the room.

"What other reasons? I am a busy man. I have things to do!" Toldnas crossed his arms on top of his distended gut and leaned back.

"I assure you that I wouldn't keep you from leaving if I didn't have something very important to share with you. I must now admit that there was a very specific reason why I chose to hold this tournament, which was the first of its kind for quite some time. My aim in holding the tournament, and breaking the fighters up into five different divisions was done so in order to gather unto myself the greatest fighters from across all of Pakk…"

"What is Pakk?" Benny asked before realizing he had spoken up.

Benny half expected the Emperor to jump all over him for his rudeness, but the great man remained cool and collected. "Pakk is the name of the world we live in. It includes everything from the Northern Mountains to the jungles of the far south, from beyond the western deserts to the islands of the east across the ocean, and much more. Since ages past, there has always been some type of trouble upon our lands. Despite the many wars, plagues, famines and injustices that are still present in our world, our kingdoms have always found a way to overcome our failings and learn from them. However, there is an evil brooding which may threaten to overthrow and enslave most, if not all of Pakk."

"What's this hogwash you're spilling on us?" The giant

laughed sarcastically.

"Hold your tongue, giant, or I'll do it for you!" Kolpak snapped.

"That won't be necessary, stalwart dwarf. We are all friends here…at least for the moment. The time to take up arms will arise soon enough without us fighting with each other. Now, as I was saying, there is a great force arising which will try to take over all of Pakk. It would seem that some of you have already experienced this on your prior journeys." The Emperor nodded towards Dale, Benny and Virtue.

"The Kudgels…and Flack!" Virtue stated.

"Oh, this is ridiculous! Pure superstition! I am no Kudgel, but I have had dealings with many of their kind in my homeland, the desert. I can assure you there is no such conspiracy." Toldnas slammed his fist on the table in anger.

"I have spies who have infiltrated the Kudgel ranks. They have confirmed my suspicions, as have my seers, who originally alerted me to this threat. I admire your eagerness to defend those you deem your allies, giant, but their danger is greater than any of you know. For several centuries now, they have been amassing a huge army, even beginning to recruit natives of Upper and Lower Sultry. If allowed to flourish unchecked, they will wipe this land bare."

"And even if that were true, who would really be to blame, Emperor? You know the origins of the Kudgels as well as any here…humans, elves, orcs, and other races… exiled from their homelands for their refusal to participate in some ludicrous, long-forgotten world. Perhaps these Kudgels are merely returning the same scorn that was shown to them."

"How dare you defend those brutes!" shouted Kolpak,

who stood and grabbed up his war hammer.

The giant stood in turn, his face contorted in anger. "Have you lived in the desert, you spoiled little dwarf? I have lived among the Kudgels and for my entire life I have seen them struggle merely to survive…I have never encountered a more hard-working people. You chastise me for defending beings you consider brutes, when in fact it was people like *you* who drove them away for their unwillingness to participate in senseless violence!"

"Nobody is here to point fingers." The Emperor stood up, stopping the argument between dwarf and giant. "I do not condone the actions of my ancestors. If what Toldnas says holds any truth, and I suspect it does, I would be more than willing to allow the Kudgels and all of the desert peoples to live freely in Upper Sultry. However, it has become clear from my network of informants that the Kudgels have no desire for peace and harmony. I am willing to compensate them for any hardships that they have endured in the centuries since their exile, but it is clear now that they have no goal other than to destroy and cause mayhem. Action must be taken. That is why I held the tournament, and why you five warriors, and my other guests, are here now. I am commissioning you lot to begin our own private army…a resistance of sorts…who will be ready when the Kudgels finally burst from their hiding places. It is only a matter of time."

"Only a matter of time before tyrants like *you* get what's coming to you!" shouted Toldnas. "You don't have the right to raise one finger against the Kudgels after what your kind has done to them!"

This time Dale stood. "Nobody is excusing what happened to your people. The Kudgels have a right to be repaid for what was unjustly taken away from them in years past. If you'd pull your head out of your, um…butt…you'd realize that the Emperor isn't trying to argue against this. If the Kudgels came forward in the open, in peace, as a civilized people, they would be greeted with respect. But, I have encountered their kind, and I agree with the Emperor that they have no desire for anything other than murder and mayhem. Several attempts on my life, and my friends, are testament to that."

"If they made attempts on your life, thunder dick, I'm sure they were for good reason!" Toldnas shouted.

"Why are you so angry? If you know the Kudgels have no conspiracy against Pakk, why not act as the middle man, and prevent even more needless catastrophe instead of yelling and judging?" the Emperor asked, raising his hands in one last attempt to bring peace to the situation.

"To hell with you, to hell with peace, and to hell with Pakk!"

Before anyone could react, Toldnas ripped open his cloak to reveal the reason for his distended gut: Red Rat Flack had strapped himself to the giant's midsection and had been eavesdropping the entire time. Flack jumped off his ally and two daggers appeared in his hands. While Toldnas took on Dale, Helena, and the other warriors, Flack made straight for the Emperor. Benny rushed to intervene, but Flack was too fast. Before the assassin could be blocked by two guards, he threw the daggers with deadly speed and accuracy right at the Emperor's neck. Benny could only watch in horror as the Son of the Sun sat helpless in his chair.

Chapter 13

All was lost. Flack's daggers would strike their mark before Benny or anyone else could react. Time seemed to stand still; the blades inched their way towards the Emperor's neck. Flack frog-leaped over the guards trying to stop him – not that it would help the Emperor now – and charged towards the ruler of Upper Sultry to see the killing through. Benny jumped from his chair as fast as he could, grabbing the staff he had won for his victory in the tournament. But he was too slow. Even if he took Flack out, the blades would still kill the Emperor. Then suddenly, a gust of wind emanated from the seated ruler, and his face became illuminated with light.

"Enough!" he shouted.

The daggers disintegrated just as they were about to reach the Emperor. He shot up out of his seat and thrust the palm of his right hand towards Flack. The assassin stopped as if he'd ran into a brick wall, and was then thrown back over twenty feet across the room. Benny could hear Flack squeal as he landed near the entrance to the dining hall. He was only winded, though, and retreated through the doors and into the hallway. Several guards ran after him, and were gone as well.

"Are you ok, sire?" Benny asked.

The Emperor gave a sly grin. "That wasn't the first attempt on my life and it certainly won't be the last."

"Give us a hand lad!" Kolpak screamed at Benny.

Benny turned to witness Dale, Helena and Kolpak fighting the desert giant. Many times their weapons met their mark, but the sheer size of Toldnas prevented blows from being anything more than flesh wounds. Quill had flown up onto the giant's shoulders and was repeatedly striking him in the neck with a dagger the Sorai had snatched from the giant's waist. Toldnas grabbed the pestering Quill and slammed him hard onto the stone floor. Meanwhile, Virtue had assumed bat form, and flew around the combatants, giving them strength, speed, and healing bites as needed. However, the giant's fighting prowess was far beyond that of the entire group combined. Benny looked at the Emperor, knowing that the ruler had enough power to stop Toldnas in his tracks.

"Use the staff!" the Emperor stated.

"But how?" What good would a mere stick do?

"The staff is imbued with great magic. It will do as you command. Use it against Toldnas! Your friends may not last much longer."

The Emperor was right. Kolpak had been delivered a nasty cut on his right leg, which even Virtue could not heal. Dale was too tired from the tournament to assume berserker mode, and despite Helena's prowess with a sword the giant was too large and powerful for her. Most of the guards had gone after Flack, and the few that remained were too flustered to help, and merely stood as spectators, waiting for the giant to finish off his current enemy and move on to them. Benny looked at the staff he held in his hands. He had never used a magical weapon before, and he had no time to ask for tips from the Emperor. Knowing nothing else to do, he raised the gnarled end of the staff and pointed it in Toldnas' direction. *Stop Toldnas!* Benny willed the stick. Benny's arm then lurched back as a beam of light shot out of the tip of his staff, passed harmlessly through Dale, and struck Toldnas directly in the forehead. The giant reeled on his feet for a few seconds, and then dropped to the ground dead.

"What the...?" Helena dropped her sword to her side and turned to Benny.

"I...I..." Benny still held the staff, smoke pouring from the tip.

Dale had suffered a nasty cut between his eyebrows, which bled profusely. Were it not for the fact that he'd been missing his nose already, Benny would have thought he had just been maimed. The Emperor rested a mighty hand on Benny's shoulder and spoke for the flustered, scar-mouthed warrior.

"The walking staff he chose is imbued with a powerful magic. It can only react to the commands of those who wield it. I told the boy to use the staff. Had he not reacted quickly enough, I would have stopped Toldnas."

"Thanks for the wait, Ben." Dale looked annoyed, but Helena punched him on the shoulder. "But I do thank you for helping us. Just try to react a bit faster next time."

He ripped off the sleeve of his shirt and tied it tightly around Kolpak's bleeding thigh. Virtue assumed human form again, and quickly changed back into the clothes she had hastily thrown off in the transformation. "He was strong."

"Giants usually are," Kolpak said, holding Dale's bled-through shirt sleeve against his cut. "I need a medic, quickly."

The Emperor raised his hands. "That won't be necessary." The bleeding on Kolpak's leg ceased, and as the dwarf took off the bandage the group was shocked to see that the cut had completely scarred over.

Everyone looked shocked, but the Emperor continued speaking. "Toldnas and Flack are prime examples of the truth behind what I speak of. We must begin our countermeasures now."

"Then let us hunt them out like the rats they are!" Kolpak heaved his hammer into the air.

The Emperor was unimpressed. "No, that's exactly what the Kudgels want, for us to wreak havoc by engaging in an open war. We'll be accomplishing their own objectives for them. No, to openly seek them out would only add fuel to their flame of mayhem, and it would cause havoc across all of Pakk. We must beat them at their own game. That is where these come in…"

He motioned for one of his guards to step forward. The guard passed a small golden whistle to each of the tournament victors, as well as to Virtue and Quill. Aside from the precious metal of its substance it was quite plain, apart from a small ruby-like gem embedded on the top of each whistle.

"What are we gonna do with these? Play them a lullaby?" Kolpak tossed his whistle onto the table.

"These are tools which will play a big part in the building of our own private army. These are special whistles; they will activate the beacon gems which you will pass out, in secret, to your allies. If and when the Kudgels strike, you will blow this whistle, activate the beacons, and alert our allies that our enemy is on the move. They will expect to come upon us unawares, like thieves in the night. But they are the ones who will be in for a surprise."

"Can you demonstrate?" Quill asked.

A guard brought a medium sized bag and set it down on the dining table. He pulled out a handful of small diamond-like gemstones. The Emperor took one of the golden whistles to his mouth and blew lightly. The gemstones became lit by a bright blue light, but that was not all. Benny could feel his attention completely attuned to the gems and the demonstration at hand. These gem-beacons were magically imbued to attract the attention of the one who possessed them to whatever their purpose was.

"You come from all over Pakk. Bags of whistles and gems will be given to each of you. I will give you magical bags which will shrink in size to prove more practical for travel and won't attract attention. Pass them out only to your most trusted allies. If someone blows a whistle, the magic inside the gems will tell you exactly where the beacon is being activated from."

"We'll spread the word in Lower Sultry," Dale said, gesturing to himself and his companions.

"I'll make ready my tribe in the north," Kolpak said.

"And I will spread the word amongst Sorais in the northwest." Quill saluted with his whistle.

"I am going to remain with Dale and my new friends," Helena said, "but I'll pass on my whistle to my sister Amazons and they will take it to the deep south."

"Good. If any of the whistles are blown, the gems on your fellows' whistles will likewise act as beacons so that you will not be left to doubt." The Emperor returned to his seat and rested his chin on his fists, reflecting on the events of the night.

Dale walked around to where his comrades were standing around the body of the slain giant. Aside from Kolpak's cut, which the Emperor had healed, the group was free of injury aside from a few scrapes and bruises.

"Hold on to that staff, kid. It'll prove useful." Dale put his arm around Benny's shoulder. "And good shot with Toldnas. It reminded me of Kidneywart."

Quill stepped forward to bid farewell to the travelers. "I have a long flight ahead of me if I plan to get home soon enough to alert my people. It was a pleasure to fight both against and beside you, Dale. I hope we meet again."

"You can bet on that!" Dale shook his hand and the Sorai left.

"What about you, Kolpak?" Virtue asked the dwarf.

"I think I can afford to stay a night longer in the city, if my pass doesn't wear off before then." He held up his blue hand. "Can't say I'll miss it."

Kolpak bid the group farewell and safe journeys before leaving for an inn downtown. The Emperor shook the hands of the quartet, but before Benny could follow his comrades, the Emperor stopped him.

"You have the eyes of one who has conversed with the Protector."

"What…how…?" Benny stammered.

"You think you're the only one who has been blessed by the Almighty? Though the circumstances of our histories differ, I have experienced many hardships and blessings. I've lost loved ones, and witnessed atrocities that would sicken a demon. It seems that you've already experienced some of these things, am I right?"

Benny's hand rose to his own scarred face. He looked

down, but the Emperor lifted his head up with a large finger.

"Don't be ashamed of your past. It is behind you, and unless you know time travel, which is a very rare thing these days, there's nothing you can do about it." The Emperor smiled.

Benny gazed at the fallen giant across the room. Sorrow filled his heart. He realized that this had been the first time he had ever truly killed a living creature (not counting zombies) and he hated the feeling it left him with. The Emperor seemed to sense the boy's feelings of remorse, and comforted him.

"Murder, even when justified, is wrong. Mercy should be sought above all else; however, as is the case with Toldnas, there are some people whose only goal in life is to maim, murder and destroy. These people cannot be reasoned or bartered with. It is a sad truth, but sometimes fatal force must be used in these circumstances."

Benny felt better, but was still confused. "I've seen the Protector, and know he exists. But I don't understand. Why would he allow these kinds of atrocities among his own creations?"

"It wasn't always like this," the Emperor said. "There was a time when all that existed was peace and prosperity among all races of creatures. But peace was not in our hearts, and we turned against the will of the Protector."

"Then why doesn't he stop us? Why doesn't he just snap his fingers and start things fresh?"

"And how long do you think it would last, young Benny? The Protector is not a tyrant. He will never force one of his creatures to believe Him or follow His ways. Nobody wants anything to do with the divine, yet when things don't go their way they all begin to hate, doubt, and criticize.

Their reaction would be quite similar, if not worse, if the Protector didn't allow this freedom of decision. They would hate him regardless." The Emperor, finished, walked back to the door he had entered through.

"It's been so long since I have felt his presence. The more time that passes, the more I feel that the Protector has abandoned me," Benny said.

The Emperor stopped in his tracks, but didn't turn around. "Silence is not the same as absence. It's funny how we often equate the two."

Benny took a deep breath and turned, staff in hand, to catch up with his companions.

CHAPTER 14

They were nearly back to the airship docks when the quartet noticed a larger group of Amazons a way down the path. Benny recognized a few of them that had fought in the tournament, but hadn't made it past the first few rounds. Helena rolled her eyes and looked to her new companions.

"Let me go explain things to them. They are my tribal sisters," she said.

"I thought you were alone. That was the reason you asked to stay at my house, wasn't it?" Dale was perplexed.

"Well, that wasn't particularly true. They temporarily shunned me from the group for getting drunk and starting trouble with a bouncer at the inn in Bluecorn Betty. My punishment was not being allowed to lodge with them for the duration of the trip."

Benny chuckled, "That was you who fought Marty?"

"He packed a good punch," she said, "but my sisters aren't so stubborn as to ignore a task like the one the Emperor bestowed upon us. I might as well get it over with."

She walked over to the group and began speaking with a muscular woman sporting a Mohawk. Benny found himself staring once again at the ripped, half-naked physiques of the two conversing Amazons. Helena's 'sister' caught Benny staring and made an obscene gesture towards him, grabbing her crotch and biting the air like a wild animal. Virtue and Dale burst out laughing. Helena came back and slapped Benny on the shoulder.

"That's Helga. I think she has the hots for you." Helena winked.

"Well she can keep dreaming." Benny began to blush as he quickly grabbed Virtue's hand, attempting to avert the distant Amazon's gaze. Even worse was the playfully chastising gaze of Virtue. Benny was eager to change the topic.

"You tell them what's up?" Benny asked.

"Yes. I gave them my whistle and a bag of gems. They will do their part." Helena resumed her walk beside Dale.

They reached the dock where the gondola of Dale's airship was anchored, and Benny saw Purp standing at attention by the compartment door. He had his usual sour face, and while he remained respectful towards Dale, it was clear he wanted no part of his master's companions. Benny remembered the story Dale had told him about Purp's upbringing, and approached him alone in hopes of relating with him.

"I just wanted to thank you for all you've done," Benny said.

Purp looked annoyed that Benny was delaying him from his duties as ship captain. "Please don't thank me. It's my duty." Benny wasn't making any headway, so he spoke up again.

"Dale told me about what happened to you. My parents both died while I was young, too. I know what it feels to be alone." Benny smiled and moved to shake the butler's hand.

Purp met him with a steely gaze. "If I require sympathy from you I'll ask for it!"

The polka-dotted man stormed out of the cabin and made way for the cockpit. Dale had noticed what Benny said, and shook his head.

"I was just trying to be grateful," Benny said.

"He doesn't like being coddled, Ben. He's a proud man." Dale crossed his arms as he leaned back on a lounge chair.

"Whatever." Benny walked over to the bed where Virtue had passed out, and fell down beside her.

The gondola shook as the airship detached from the dock and headed back out the main gate to the Imperial City. Benny and Virtue dozed in their beds while Helena sat in Dale's lap; they both snored loudly. If it hadn't been for the events that had transpired that day at the feast, Benny would've complained.

They made it back to Dale's mansion and, after some complaints from Purp about them dirtying the ship's cabin, they retired to their rooms for the continuance of their nap. The next morning they ate a hearty breakfast and Dale told Purp what happened at the feast with the Emperor. Purp seemed unusually concerned as Dale told him about the Kudgel threat and the beacons, and was all too eager to disperse some beacons among the other servants and neighboring estates.

"I don't trust him as far as I can throw him," Virtue whispered to Benny as they ate pancakes.

"I don't either, but Dale likes him and Purp seems to at least respect Dale. Besides, he's just a butler. What could he do, forget to change out bed sheets?" Benny thought for a split second that Purp had heard the last remark, but the servant didn't seem to notice.

They left the next day after saying farewell to Purp and the other inhabitants of Dale's estate, including the gnome village. They walked a long ways before finally reaching the hill where the group had teleported to Upper Sultry.

"How exactly are we supposed to teleport back? There's nothing…"

Benny's question ended abruptly as he walked right into a brick wall. He looked around at the building that had popped out of thin air. It was in fact the wizard's cabin on Siegfried's Belltower, transplanted onto the top of the grassy hill.

"It only appears as you get closer to it." Dale opened the door and they entered.

The Wizard looked up from a book of magic when they entered. "Back so soon? You haven't been gone a week. You sure ya'll don't want to stick around and see the sights?"

"No time." Dale gave a quick rundown of the Kudgel conspiracy.

"Wow, Nelly! Too much info for me! Leave me out of it!" The Wizard cupped his hands over his ears.

"But if the Kudgels attack, Siegfried's Bell won't be safe. Don't you care about your own safety?" Virtue asked.

"What are you talking about, you stupid vampire? Of course I care for my safety. You think I'm some pickle-headed idiot? If something happens, my assistant and I will scurry off and hide like the good little mice we are."

"You're a coward!" Helena exclaimed.

"You don't know the half of it," Dale said.

"Let's just teleport back to Lower Sultry," Benny said,

making for the stairs to the clapper.

"Oh…that won't be possible, sorry Jim," the Wizard said.

Dale reached for his sword, nobody bothering to stop him. "Why the hell not?"

The purple-haired dwarf looked down from where he sat in his loft-bed. "Because it's our day off, dummy!"

Dale shouted incoherently and a gust of wind shot forth from his mouth, knocking the dwarf out of his place in the rafters of the cabin. It would appear that lightning wasn't the only element Dale's mage-cry could summon. The Wizard seemed unimpressed.

"Kill us. That's fine by me. Then you'll have to make the long trek to Lower Sultry on foot. Only I know how to work this place."

"Damn." Dale knew the Wizard was right.

"We can't afford that, Dale. We need to get back as soon as possible to start warning people," Helena said.

"Ok…what'll it take?" Dale asked.

The dwarf grumbled something from across the room and the Wizard smiled. "Well, I guess I could do it for a small amount of gold. However, you've inconvenienced me with that little summer breeze a moment ago. My assistant may prove unruly for quite some time if you don't repent."

Dale rolled his eyes and turned to the dwarf. "What do you want, you purple-haired freak?!"

"I want the vampire to do what she did the last time, except this time I wanna do it with her," the dwarf pointed to Helena.

"Why you little…!" Dale began to charge the dwarf, but Helena stopped him.

"It's a deal," Helena said. "Why should the vampire

have all the fun?"

The dwarf hopped back up into his bed as Virtue gave him the bite, which would begin the hallucinogenic love sequence with the Amazon. As the dwarf began to snore lightly, a wide grin spread across his face. The Wizard waved his hands in the air and a bubble, similar to before, appeared over the dwarf's head, revealing the vision for all to see. The dwarf was bound and gagged, doggy style, to a table as the naked Helena stood behind him cracking a whip against his hairy buttocks.

Some fun, Benny thought.

"Oooh, I didn't know he was into that freaky stuff… wow, honey, you sure can…" The Wizard stopped when he saw the aggravated look on the scarred man's face.

"Jealousy does not become you," Helena murmured to Dale, smiling.

"Let's get this over with." Dale led the group up to the clapper, where they found four seats this time, repeated the same annoying **Bong** of the bell, and returned to the cabin, being once again on top of the spire of Bluecorn Castle.

"Thanks again for visiting Siegfried's Bell! Do come again!" The Wizard called as they ascended back down to the boardwalks of the township.

They visited the inn and tavern, where they found Marty and Bum. They explained the entirety of the events that had transpired since leaving Bluecorn Betty. Marty was at first skeptical to their tale, but he trusted Dale and agreed to alert as many people in the surrounding areas as he could.

"I've got quite a few friends in these parts. I'll spread the word," he said.

Since Virtue didn't intend to leave Benny's side any time soon, she gave Marty her whistle to signal the beacons in case the Kudgels struck Bluecorn Betty first. They bid farewell to Marty once again, and Bum rejoined them as they made way for Dan. Bum didn't seem as intimidated to meet Helena as the others had been, but then again, he was an orc. Dale picked up the wagon and mule from the man he'd paid to watch them, and they made way for Dan. Things seemed normal, but Benny could feel the evil force growing; every time he closed his eyes the green eye was there, waiting for him. It was only a matter of time before the Kudgels would strike.

CHAPTER 15

Benny was tired. Their group, consisting of himself and Virtue, Dale and Helena, and Bum, had finally made it back to Gant, passing out beacons and whistles to several settlements along the way. They had visited the giant Liverwart and given him a beacon set. It had been easy enough, except that the folk they met were not universally accepting of their warning, so there was some emotional stress.

But mainly it was Benny's recurring nightmare of the green eye and tentacles that burned into him and squeezed him painfully. At first the dream had been occasional, but now it was becoming regular. Virtue knew of it, and quickly woke him when it caught him, but that was only temporary relief. It claimed to be the Grand Exalted Cyclops, the leader of the invading Kudgels. But wasn't Flack the leader? This didn't feel like Flack. And what would the Cyclops want with Benny, anyway? Benny was just a minor cog in a much larger effort of organization.

Was the Cyclops sending hateful messages to many prospective opponents, and Benny was just one of hundreds? That didn't seem right either; no one he had encountered had mentioned anything similar. So it seemed that Benny was the only one. Why? It just didn't seem to make much sense. Regardless, it was tearing him up.

"What can I do?" he cried to Virtue. "It's driving me crazy! I need to get clear of this horror, but I don't know how."

"There must be a reason it is persecuting you," Virtue said. "You must represent a serious danger to it."

"And Dale doesn't? Helena doesn't? The Emperor doesn't? You don't? Why should a minor figure like me deserve such special attention?"

She shook her head. "Only the Protector knows."

"The Protector! The one I called Search? He said he'd be there when I needed him, but I haven't seen him recently. I don't think he's interested."

"Maybe he prefers to be asked," she said gently.

Benny stared at her. Did she mean to pray? Well, it wouldn't hurt to try. Then he looked inward. *Protector, I am asking.*

A single ward came to him. *Magenta.*

"Magenta?" he repeated aloud.

"That is a purplish red color," Virtue said.

"It's what the Protector told me, I think. But how would that, or any other color, help me?"

"I don't know. Maybe Dale would know; he's been around more than we have." She got up and went to find Dale.

Benny feared that they were being foolish. Maybe his imagination had produced a random word, just to shut him up, as it were. It might have no meaning at all.

Virtue returned. "Dale knew!" she exclaimed. "It's a person! A person with magenta colored hair, face, hands, and feet. The rest of her is green."

"I have to find a green girl with purplish red hair?"

"Yes! Because her name is Magenta."

"What does she have to do with the price of beans in Gant?"

"She is Purp's lost sister."

That might make sense. Purp was purple, so his sister could be a different shade of purple. The one who declined Dale's offer of comfortable residence, and was said to make her living as a prostitute.

"The whore?"

"What she does to survive is no necessary indication of her character."

Benny realized that she was quietly reproving him for his prejudice. As a vampire, she had suffered from prejudice herself. "Still, how does she relate to me, if she does?"

"We don't know, but Dale and Helena think it is beyond coincidence that you should come up with her name, when you didn't know it. We need to know how she relates. It could be important."

"I asked the Protector for help dealing with the Cyclops. How is this relevant?"

Virtue smiled. "Only the Protector knows. It is for us to find out."

Benny still suspected it was coincidence, but maybe that was better than nothing. "How do we find out? Do we go see her?"

"That would require another teleport to Upper Sultry. That might be complicated. The dwarf might demand to spend an amorous night with *you*."

Benny winced. Even in the dwarf's dream, that did not appeal. "So do we send her a letter?"

"No, that would take too much time and we might not get an answer. Helena says she'll help."

"How?"

"She thinks we can contact Magenta telepathically."

"The Amazon is telepathic?"

"No. But her blood is special."

"About the price of beans in Gant..."

"You'll see. We are in excellent luck. There is a vamp telepath near Gant. He goes by the designation Tele, preferring anonymity in other respects."

"But you're telepathic. Who needs him?"

"I am a minor short range telepath. I can track you a fair distance, but not a stranger as far away as Magenta is. This one is a full telepath. He has the range that I lack. He should be able to reach Magenta."

"And ask her why her name came into my head? She might think I was looking for her, um, business."

"Not if Helena contacts her."

"Why should she do that? I'm the one haunted by the Cyclops."

"Which is the main reason. The Cyclops is orienting on you, not Helena. If you contact Magenta, the green eyeball may know and mess it up. But Helena should be able to do it without alerting it."

"And why should Helena do that for me?" he asked again.

"Because you were the one who cut apart the forbidding knot of honor and gave her Dale to love. Also, she has a feeling about this that goes beyond mere curiosity. She thinks it's expedient. Something she should do."

Benny shrugged. "Then let's do it."

Soon the four of them walked to the house of the

vampire telepath, some distance in the woods beyond Gant. Virtue mentally signaled him they were coming, and why, and he agreed. Benny suspected that even purely mentally she came across as a lovely creature, one any man would be happy to do a favor for.

"Come in, party of four," Tele said. He did not conceal his fangs, as they already knew his nature. Benny was sure he normally preferred to be anonymous, because vampires were generally distrusted. Virtue, however, had done much to alleviate that locally; everyone liked her. "My, you ladies are lovely, both of you."

"Thank you," Virtue and Helena said almost together.

"I can't say the same for you men," Tele said with a smile.

"Thank you," Benny and Dale said almost together, laughing. Benny found that he liked this man.

"I see that this is one I must do pro bono."

"We prefer to pay you," Dale said. "It is private business."

"Allow me to clarify. I am a superior telepath. I read all minds in my vicinity." He smiled briefly. "That is part of what protects me from ignorant vigilantes. I do charge for private business, but yours is actually a private aspect of public business. You seek to stop the invasion of the Kudgel horde, something I had not known about until very recently. It seems that the leader of that horde considers Benny to be a menace to their effort, so he is trying to discourage Benny in an unobtrusive manner. That is, mentally rather than physically, so there are no physical fingerprints. There must be a reason the Cyclops has not simply sent an assassin. Helping Benny to avoid that discouragement therefore becomes a public service. You believe that this woman Magenta may be the key to this avoidance. I do not see how, but the nature of the contact with the Protector is persuasive. It behooves me to assist you, and to keep your secrets. I will help you interview Magenta."

The four shared a glance. This was one potent telepath!

Tele smiled. "Besides, I am not interested in tasting any Amazon blood."

They laughed. He knew about what Helena's blood could do to a vampire.

"And it must be the Amazon," Tele continued. "Because the Cyclops evidently does not yet know about her participation in your campaign. However, I may be able to include the others on a peripheral basis."

"Peripheral?" Dale asked.

"The Amazon will be the lead figure, governing the interview, but the others may participate. They merely will not register if another telepath snoops."

"You can do that?" Helena asked. "Bring them along as astral spectators?"

"With my assistance," Virtue said. "Which, of course, I will provide." She blushed. Benny wondered why.

"He just wants to get into your pretty mind," Helena said.

Tele laughed. "Ah, you caught me! Given a choice between a lovely body and a lovely mind, I do prefer the mind."

Ah, mind dating. Benny distrusted this, remembering the sexual appetites of the dwarf. Virtue laid her hand on his. "It is legitimate intimacy," she said. "Unavoidable, for this. We must interleave our minds."

And, of course, he trusted her. The dwarf had never actually touched her or Helena, physically.

Tele closed his eyes, concentrating. "I have located Magenta. The timing is propitious. She is currently between clients."

Just like that!

"Make yourselves comfortable," Tele said. "We shall proceed."

Then Benny realized that he was going into a dream state, as were the others. Virtue was doing it, borrowing Tele's superior power to augment her own. She was linking their minds so that they could experience what Helena did. As "astral spectators." Tele was connecting them to the distant Magenta.

Then they were seated in a sequestered hovel. Blankets hung on cords formed the walls, lending privacy to the central bed. Overturned empty wine-kegs made the chairs, and a covered bucket was the toilet. It was what some preferred to call a minimalist residence.

A striking woman looked up from the basin where she was rinsing her hands. Her loosely robed body was deep green, while her face, hair, hands, and feet were reddish purple. This was clearly Magenta. "Well, hello, you several folk," she said, surprised. "Is this a vision?"

"It is a vision," Helena agreed. "But we are real, in a distant place. We are catching you between trysts, as it were, so as not to disturb your livelihood. We will depart soon."

"So you know my business," Magenta said. Her eyes were green, matching her body. She was actually a beautiful, if colorful, woman, whose northerly and southerly assets peeked out tantalizingly from behind the robe, by no coincidence. Benny and Dale were both staring; they could not help it.

"We know it," Helena said. "And do not condemn

you for it. We all do what we must do. But we are curious about one thing: we understand that your brother Purp has an excellent job as head butler at an estate." She did not identify Dale as the owner of that estate, as that would have ruined his anonymity. "Further, that you could have joined him there, perhaps as a hostess, and had a very comfortable life. Why did you not do so?"

"You call him Purp? I truly care for my brother, and he cares for me," Magenta said. "But I happen to know his business, and I can't tolerate it. So I stay well away from him, and make no reference to him here."

"His business?" Helena asked. "He's a butler. There is no shame in that."

"His real business."

"I do not understand."

"It is not a thing I care to bruit about."

Benny wondered what business could be so bad that a prostitute could not abide it. And what other business could the butler be in?

"But suppose it relates to our mission here?" Helena asked.

"What is your mission here?"

"My friend," Helena glanced at Benny, not naming him. "He is suffering malign visitations by a being called the Grand Exalted Cyclops."

"The Cyclops!" Magenta repeated, startled.

"You know of him?"

"Oh, I do! But I want nothing to do with him."

Helena smiled thinly. "Nobody does, except the Kudgels he leads. We oppose them. But it seems my friend is marked for special torment. The Cyclops visits him in dreams, and threatens him. That is what we want to stop.

We received information that you might be able to help."

"I can help no more than any other citizen of Upper or Lower Sultry. It is common knowledge that spelled witch hazel can block unwanted mental intrusions. I use it myself, to keep clients out of my mind. My body is theirs to play with, but my mind is private. That makes my business bearable."

"Spelled witch hazel!" Virtue exclaimed. "I have heard of that!"

"Most vamps have," Magenta said. "Because of the way it relates to telepathy."

"I just never thought to use it for that particular purpose," Virtue said.

"It seems that we had no need to bother you," Helena said. "I apologize."

"There must be more to it," Magenta said. "However, my next appointment is incipient, so if you will excuse me--"

"One thing, please. I have an insatiable curiosity about mysteries," Helena said. "You reacted fiercely to my mention of the Cyclops. Do you know more of him?"

"I do, but that is another thing I don't care to bruit about."

"I will make a deal with you. Tell me, and I will swear to be there for you if ever you need me, to the best of my ability."

Benny remembered how the Amazon had made a similar deal with him, and honored it in spades.

Magenta considered. "This is not an offer to be taken lightly. The word of an Amazon is potent, and there could at some point be an occasion where I could use such help. I will tell, you with one proviso: you must tell no one else."

"Agreed."

"I know who the Cyclops is."

"That is something I would like to know."

"I will whisper it to you. Remember, you must not tell."

"I remember," Helena said. She got up and approached Magenta, who whispered briefly in her ear.

The Amazon's jaw dropped. "Oh my."

Then a man's voice came from beyond the curtain. "Magenta! You there? I got a hot rod ready."

"Go!" Magenta hissed.

They went. They were back with Tele.

"I wish I had not made that deal," Helena said. "What she told me explains so much, but I am sworn to silence. That means I can't act on it either, lest my actions betray the secret."

They did not press her. She had to be true to her oath, however much the rest of them wanted to know who the Cyclops was.

"Spelled witch hazel," Benny said. "Could that really do it?"

"We'll find out," Virtue said. "I will get some forthwith."

"I regret that your mission was not completely successful," Tele said.

"But it may have been," Virtue said. "Thank you for your help."

"It may indeed have been," Helena agreed.

"It was a pleasure. Your mind is lovely, Virtue."

They returned home. Virtue soon obtained spelled witch hazel, and was about to put it on Benny's head when she paused. "I just thought--" She didn't finish.

"I hate it when you think," Benny said, smiling. "I'd so much rather have you just be sweet and pretty."

She did not smile. "It's that if we use this, and it works,

and the Cyclops can no longer harass you, won't he suspect that we're on to him? That maybe we even know who he is, though it's only Helena who really does?"

"I should think so," Benny agreed. "But does it matter?"

"He must have reason to try to take you out of this campaign, but alive, as Tele said. If he can't discourage you, will he then send the assassin?"

Benny felt a chill. "Better to kill me, than allow me to mess him up, from his perspective. He must need me for something, and if he loses control of me, then yes, kill me."

She looked at the bottle of witch hazel. "I don't think we can use this."

Regretfully, Benny had to agree. "I will simply have to keep suffering, much as I hate it."

"I'm so sorry."

"But with you to comfort me, I think I can handle it."

"Thank you."

But he wondered: when he had asked the Protector for help, he had been given the name of Magenta, who had mentioned the simple remedy. Why hadn't the Protector simply sent the words Spelled Witch Hazel? Not only did he not know why the Cyclops was after him, he didn't know why the Protector had taken this somewhat devious route. What were they still missing?

"What, indeed," Virtue echoed.

Chapter 16

A few days later, a breathless messenger arrived at the Fox Den. "The Sisters Dorn are under siege by hordes of Kudgels and Kudgel converts!" he gasped.

"So it has come," Dale said grimly. "We must go to their aid."

"You're a lot of man," Helena said. "But not much of a tactician. Hasn't it occurred to you that this could be a diversion, a ploy to get us out of Gant so they can raid it with impunity?"

Dale nodded, not taking offense. "I leave it to you to achieve such occurrences. But we can't let the twin cities of Galver and Elim Dorn be ravaged. We must help them."

"We must indeed," she agreed. "But we'll have to divide our forces. Half of us can remain here to protect this region, and half can go to help the cities. Fortunately it's leadership they will need more than brute strength. Individual warriors can't hope to stop armies by themselves, no matter how competent."

"Virtue and I are a team," Benny said.

"As are Helena and I," Dale agreed. "Shall we draw lots to see who goes?"

"I will scry it," Virtue said. Soon she reported on the result. "Benny and I will go to the twin cities. That is the more favorable auspice."

"That leaves Bum," Dale said. "Where do you wish to be, friend? Here guarding the inn, or there amidst the bloodshed?"

"With the action," the orc said promptly.

"So be it," Dale agreed, unsurprised.

They activated the beacons with their own whistles, and soon all the gems they had passed out throughout the planet of Pakk were activated. Kudgels were arising all over in a coordinated campaign. The game was on.

"We need to get to Galver Dorn quickly," Benny said. "But it's a two day ride by wagon. That may be too late. Somehow I hadn't thought of that detail."

"My skry indicated we would get there in time," Virtue said.

"How? We don't have travel magic here."

"I don't know. But I trust my skry."

Benny didn't care to argue with her. He would just have to trust that however long their journey took, they would indeed arrive in time.

Virtue spoke to Bum. "We must depart within the hour. Are you ready?"

"I am ready," the orc said in his squeaky voice. He wore a compact backpack, and his weapons were strapped to his blue-green body.

Benny and Virtue got their own backpacks, and Benny strapped on his sword. He regretted that he had to leave his new magic walking stick behind, but he did not yet know how to use it well enough, and didn't want to risk losing it. There would be another day.

Dale intercepted him. "Take this too." He proffered his magic club, which looked like a small metallic rod.

"But you'll need that yourself!" Benny protested.

"I can spare it. I have other weapons."

"I'm not sure I could even heft it effectively."

"It has power steering. You can wield it." He pressed the rod into Benny's hand.

"I—I don't know what to say."

"Don't say anything. It's not verbally commanded. Merely squeeze to invoke it, and squeeze again to enhance it, and again to revert it."

That wasn't what Benny had meant, as Dale surely knew. He squeezed the rod, and it transformed into a club almost five feet long. It looked massive, but felt light in his hand. He tapped the floor with it, experimentally, and the floor cracked. The mass was there at the business end. He squeezed the handle again, and dozens of steel spikes popped out, each one several inches long. This was one deadly instrument!

"See, you already have the hang of it," Dale said approvingly.

"Uh, thank you." Benny squeezed the handle again, and the club reverted to the rod. He tucked it into his belt, overwhelmed by the loan. It would make him twice as formidable a fighter, as Dale knew.

The giant Liverwart arrived. "Messenger passed. Then beacons on," he said. "So me come."

Then Benny realized how they would travel swiftly. They had done it before, when the giant carried them. Virtue's skry had known. But one problem remained. "There's one more in our party. I don't know whether--"

"I will run," Bum said. "If Virtue bites me."

And there was the other aspect Benny had overlooked: Virtue's ability to enhance physical prowess by her bites.

"Of course," Virtue agreed. She was back to full vigor now, and her bites never depleted her noticeably anyway.

"Then I guess it's time to go," Benny said. He shook hands with Dale and Laughing Jack, then hesitated before Helena. Did one shake hands with a woman?

She grasped his hand, then drew him in so she could kiss him. She had been well disposed toward him since he untangled the geas of honor that had kept her from Dale. Still, he was surprised both by the gesture and by how hot and feminine this tattooed warrior could be when she tried.

She laughed. "You thought I would bite you? That's Virtue's department."

"Oh, okay," he said, embarrassed, not caring to clarify his actual concern. If she ever tried to seduce him, he would be hard put to it to resist. Not that she ever would, and of course he *would* resist. Still, that kiss had been surprisingly potent.

Then he saw Virtue's quirk of a smile. She was reading his mind!

Dale clapped him on the back. "I think those lady canines conspired to make you blush."

"Oh, you caught on," Helena said, faking a frown.

Then they all were laughing. It was a way to ease the tension of the deadly situation they were in.

Virtue bit Bum. "Oh, you can bite me anytime, you divine creature," the orc breathed as he flexed his muscles. She smiled; he was pretending she had given him an erotic bite instead of a power bite. It seemed that every male in the vicinity had erotic dreams of the vampire. Fortunately, she was able to handle their mental urges.

Then Virtue stepped out of her clothing, unashamed of her nudity, handed her things to Benny, transformed to bat form and perched on Benny's shoulder. Liverwart picked him up and set him on *his* shoulder. They were ready to go.

"I love that passing eyeful," Dale said.

"I'll give you a black eyeful," Helena said, pretending jealousy as they both laughed.

The giant started off, first striding, then running. The orc paced him. They achieved a velocity that was far beyond what Benny could have done on his own. The wind was fairly blowing his hair back. Benny waved to the others as they moved rapidly away from the inn.

In this manner they reached the town of Galver Dorn that afternoon, more than a day faster than would ordinarily have been the case. Benny hoped the Duke would be pleased by their early arrival. They did not much like Dijon, but he was the authority here, so they had to work with him.

They drew up at Duke Dijon's residence. They had come to help the Duke organize the defense of the town, which was under siege by the Kudgels. But it was clear even as Benny dismounted and Virtue resumed human form and dressed that there was a problem.

"You are naturally tired," Benny told the giant. "You have served well, and we will need you again soon. Lie down somewhere comfortable and get some rest now."

"Um," Liverwart agreed. He went to a large bush at the edge of the property and dropped to the ground behind it. In a moment he was snoring.

Now, to handle the problem. The Duke was not marshaling his troops. He was with a few members of his private guard. Caught unguarded by their early arrival, he was evidently packing his cart to secretly flee the town ahead of the Kudgel conquest. He was also packing most of the town's treasury.

"Traitor!" Bum exclaimed, furious at the betrayal.

"Go away, orc," the Duke snapped. "This isn't your business."

"It *is* my business," Bum said. "I came to help you fight off the Kudgels, and instead you are betraying your people." He was an orc, but there was no question where Bum's loyalty lay.

Dijon did not argue further. Instead he signaled his guards, who charged Bum with swinging swords.

The orc's own sword jumped into his hand. He parried the first guard, while Benny went after the second. The third guard, evidently confident of the result, went instead for Virtue. A pretty girl was always good for passing entertainment, voluntary or not.

That galvanized Benny. He had intended only to subdue his opponent, but the threat to Virtue alarmed him. He raised the rod and squeezed it. The club formed, feeling light in his hand. He swung it so viciously at the guard that it not only beat back the man's sword, it smashed into the face behind it. The guard dropped, dead.

For an instant Benny froze. He did not like killing, and always sought to avoid it if possible. But he *only* hesitated for an instant. He knew that while Virtue was quite capable of defending herself, she would not do so, being a pacifist. To her killing was worse than rape, even if she herself were the object of the rape.

"Halt!" Benny cried to the guard. But the man was oblivious. He grabbed Virtue by one arm while his other hand tore at her dress.

Benny's club caught him on the ear. The man fell to

the ground, unconscious.

"Are you all right?" Benny asked Virtue.

"I am," she said. "But he isn't." She was looking at the fallen guard.

Benny checked the man. He was worse than unconscious. His skull was fractured and he was dead. Benny had underestimated the brutal power of the club. "Sorry about that," Benny said, meaning that he hated having her witness the killing.

Then they checked the others in combat. Bum had handily dispatched his opponent. Two or three might have been a challenge; one was not.

Meanwhile the Duke was on the wagon, urging the horse forward and away. It was too late to catch him.

Except that Virtue quickly transformed to her bat form, and flew to the horse. She landed on its head. The horse paused, startled, then came to a halt. Virtue had projected a thought into its mind, telling it to stop. The Duke was going nowhere.

"I have riches!" Dijon said, trying his next ploy. "I will pay you handsomely to let me go. You'll never achieve wealth like this in your normal existence."

"Be thankful I don't stuff your gold up your exit tube!" Bum gritted. "You deserve execution."

"Well spoken," Benny said, smiling.

There turned out to be a cell in Dijon's house, probably to hold prisoners temporarily, or for more nefarious purposes. They put the Duke there, and pocketed the key. "You're out of office," Benny said. He realized that he was presuming a lot, but he was here to provide competent leadership, and this man wasn't it.

Troops approached the house. These were the Galver

Dorn Rangers, the elite city guard. "We need to see the Duke," their captain said. "We need to organize a better defense, lest the city be overwhelmed by the Kudgels."

The man was neither cowering nor fleeing; he was trying to do his job. There was no time to do a thorough study of character; he would do.

"We caught Dijon absconding with the treasury," Benny said. "We have deposed him. I hereby make a field promotion. You are the next Duke. Organize your defense; the resources of the city are yours to marshal. After this is over, the city elders will decide whether to make your ascension permanent."

The man didn't even blink. "I will get it done."

"We need to check Elim Dorn as well," Benny said. "We leave the defense of Galver in your hands."

"Yes." The man turned and signaled his detachment. He was already on the job.

"Liverwart!" Benny called.

The giant roused himself and rejoined them. Virtue bit Bum again, then transformed back to bat form. Soon they were on their way to the sister city.

Authority becomes you, Virtue thought. *You handled that well.*

Only then did Benny realize how decisive he had been. "You bolstered me telepathically!" he said.

I could not have done it had there not been good material to work with.

He hoped that was true.

They had not actually seen the invaders at Galver Dorn, as the enemy had been ravaging the other side of the city. Elim Dorn was another matter. Virtue flew up to survey the town from a distance, and reported that the situation was bad: the Kudgels were attacking, and there was also a pack of werewolves, their allies. The city had been wiped out by zombies several years before, and had recovered only partially; it was in poor shape to fend off this siege. This was going to be brutal.

We can't put Liverwart into this, Virtue thought. *He did not come here to fight, and he's tired from carrying us.*

That was true. "Where can he sleep safely?" Benny sub-vocalized.

I saw a zombie cemetery not far from town. The zombies are gone, dissolved into dirt, but there remains an odor that repels. I can bite him so it smells like roses to him. No one will bother him there.

"That should do it," Benny agreed.

They guided the giant to the zombie cemetery and dismounted, Virtue returning to human form. "You need more rest," Benny told him. "You did not come here to fight werewolves. Sleep here, and if we do not return by tomorrow morning, return to Gant alone and tell them that the twin cities may be lost."

Liverwart didn't think to argue. He sniffed the air. "Ugh!"

"That smell will protect you as you sleep," Benny said. "Virtue will make it nice for you. Hold out your hand to her."

"Okay." Liverwart reached down toward the vampire. Like all males, he liked her aspect and her touch.

Virtue bit him on the tip of a finger. He sniffed again. "Roses!" He lay down and slept, smiling.

"Now it's our turn," Benny said grimly. "We can't reason with these creatures. We'll simply have to kill them. I hate it, but see no alternative."

"I agree," Bum said.

"As you know, I can't fight," Virtue said. "But I will help you in any way I can." It wasn't just that she was a slight figure of a woman, it was that she had been raised a pacifist, and though intellectually she appreciated the need sometimes for violence, it was not in her to be violent herself. That was part of why he loved her; she was truly nice. If only all the world of Pakk were like her, what a paradise it would be!

"Thank you," she answered his thought. "But universal pacifism really is not practical. There is need also for those capable of violence, like you."

"Thank you, I think. Can you use your telepathy to give us some protection?" Benny asked.

"I can't give you physical protection, but maybe I can stop them from seeking you."

"Do that, then."

Virtue bit them each lightly in turn, kissing them in the process. Bum was embarrassed but pleased, and of course Benny was used to it. "They will see you, but not try to engage."

"How is that? They're in attack mode."

Her gaze flickered to the cemetery. "You both now have the mental aura of dead zombies."

Dead zombies. Both Benny and Bum laughed. That would do. It sounded like an oxymoron, but actually made sense, because normal zombies were half alive. They smelled even worse when they became completely dead. The two of them had the same protection Liverwart did.

"But it is only an aversion," Virtue warned them. "When you actually engage, they will ignore the odor and fight you, as they would if attacked by zombies. So don't attack them unless you have to."

They gripped their weapons and advanced on the nearest house that was under siege by three werewolves.

Virtue returned to bat form and flew unobtrusively from tree to tree, observing them without putting herself at risk.

"Okay, one gesture, to make it official," Benny said. He raised his voice. "Wolves! Cease and desist! Clear out and return where you came from, to live in peace hereafter, and we will let you go."

A wolf transformed to human form. "You and what army?" he demanded contemptuously.

Just as expected. "Are you declining to depart in peace?"

"As if you needed to ask." The man returned to wolf form, and he and his two companions charged.

"Did you really think they would leave off just because you asked them?" Bum asked.

"No. I just wanted to give them the chance, in fairness."

Bum laughed. "Werewolves are known for mayhem rather than fairness."

Then the three wolves were upon them—and sheared off, snorting. They had whiffed the stench, and thought they were up against zombies. Biting zombies was not only repulsive, it was useless. Then, realizing it was a ruse, they whirled and returned to the attack.

Benny smote the first with his magic club. The creature collapsed, his skull crushed. The second, undeterred, leaped right over his fallen companion and came at Benny through the air. His snout was driven back into his neck so that it looked as if he were headless with teeth on his chest.

Bum neatly chopped the third wolf's head off so that it fell to one side while the body plowed into the ground on the other side.

The door of the besieged house opened. "You rescued us!" the pretty housewife exclaimed, her fair hair flouncing. "How can we ever thank you?"

"Just stay inside and on guard," Benny said seriously. "There are more wolves to deal with. It is not yet safe outside."

"Oh, of course," she said, evidently disconcerted. "You are too noble." Then she caught a whiff of zombie, and hastily obliged.

She gives you too much credit for noble abstinence, Virtue's thought came. *She didn't know your wife was watching.*

"I wasn't tempted anyway," Benny muttered. "I didn't even notice how pretty she was, or how her full blouse was missing buttons."

She laughed mentally, knowing he was teasing her back.

They moved on to the next house, and the next, dispatching the wolves they encountered, lifting the sieges.

Then they came to the downtown area. The citizens had formed a cordon, piling furniture, bricks and bodies in the streets and defending them with rocks, spears and bows. They were obviously not practiced warriors, but desperation made them effective, and the invaders were balked. The end, however, seemed inevitable, because this was not merely werewolves; a Kudgel contingent was in charge.

Until Benny and Bum came on the scene. "Ghaaa!" they shouted together, and charged the back of the Kudgel line, whirling their deadly swords. In moments a half dozen Kudgels were dead on the pavement, and a similar number of wolves.

This disconcerted the Kudgels, and their line broke. The Elim defenders cheered, seeing rescue at hand.

Then the Kudgel command took hold. They formed a new line, in a circle around the two, closing in. There were too many, too closely packed, to take out readily with the swords.

But they didn't know what they were up against. Benny and Bum switched to clubs. Bum had muscle and Benny had magic. They stood back to back and swept their clubs forward, bashing heads wholesale. Soon the closing circle was a ring of bodies.

Meanwhile the townsmen, freed from the immediate pressure of the siege, rebounded, and were advancing against the invaders. It was a melee. Benny and Bum kept fighting, careful not to bash any humans, following where the battle led. They were winning!

But also tiring. There just seemed to be more and more wolves and Kudgels swarming in. They found themselves hemmed in, surrounded by bodies piled like sandbags, with others still coming on.

The zombie aura is fading. I'm coming in. It was Virtue in bat form.

Benny held up his hand. She landed on it and bit it. She hopped to Bum and bit him too. Then she flew away, just before the Kudgel archers were able to orient on her. The archers had not been able to focus on Benny and Bum, because they were so thickly beset by wolves and Kudgels and in constant motion, but a figure in the sky was another matter.

"What is this?" Bum asked, feeling the effect of the new bite.

"It's the berserker bite. We'd better separate, lest in our ferocity we harm each other."

"Got it."

They sprang apart and re-entered the fray with doubled ferocity, laying waste the entire contingent. The Kudgels kept coming, and kept dying. Benny only hoped there would not be so many that they outlasted the hour of berserker power.

A Kudgel and a werewolf came at him together, high and low, carefully coordinating. They knew what they were doing; they were a team. Even as a berserker he could not avoid both at once.

Magic, do your thing! he thought, hoping this ploy would work. If it didn't, he was dead.

He smashed the club down on the wolf's head, crushing it. At the same time the Kudgel's sword swung at his neck. The pair was willing to sacrifice one of them in order to take out this enemy. They had probably tried it before, and won without the sacrifice.

The sword swished through without contact as the neck briefly ghosted. Ready for this, Benny swung his club directly from the wolf's head to the Kudgel's knee. There was a crack as it splintered the bone. The Kudgel dropped, screaming, yet still wielding his sword; he was a real fighter. But he was out of position, and Benny's next swing took out his head.

Then, suddenly, it was over. Bodies were mounded everywhere, and the townsmen were mopping up the last of the invaders. They had won.

But when Benny found Bum, he was on the ground and near death. One of the Kudgel/werewolf teams had gotten him. Both of them were dead, but in their sacrifice they had chopped off Bum's head quills and stabbed him in the chest.

Virtue flew in and gave him a healing bite, but it wasn't enough. He had already lost too much blood. He would still die within hours.

"Fetch Liverwart," Benny told her.

Virtue flew off. Benny faced the townsmen. "You can handle it from here, can't you?"

"We can," a man agreed. "Thanks to you and the orc and the bat. We never saw the like before. There will not be much prejudice against orcs or bats, here, after this." The others nodded agreement.

"You do have to know the good ones from the bad ones," Benny said. "The same goes for giants. This one is ours." He gestured to Liverwart, who was now striding in, the bat on his shoulder. "Take him to the clerics in Galver Dorn," he said as the giant arrived.

The giant picked up the orc. Virtue gave Benny one more bite, this one for endurance. Then Liverwart strode rapidly away, and Benny ran beside him.

They made it to Galver Dorn by evening. The troops there had succeeded in beating off the Kudgels, but there had been severe losses and there were many injured and wounded people to care for. Their resources were spread thin, their medicines almost exhausted; there was little they could do for Bum. Worse, there was bad news.

"We have word the Kudgels are attacking Gant, and it is not going well," the Captain of the Guard, now the Duke, told him. "You are needed back there."

"We can't leave Bum here to die," Virtue protested.

The Captain shrugged. "We understand your distress; we share it. We simply are unable to do more."

They had to make a quick decision. Benny made it. "Liverwart, can you travel well enough in the night?"

"Can," the giant agreed.

"Then go back alone to support your friends. Virtue and I will stay here until Bum is stable enough to be left. Then we'll rejoin you in Gant."

"Will," Liverwart agreed. He set off immediately.

Now Virtue tended to Bum, biting him lightly to ease

the pain and enable him to sleep. Benny relaxed, letting his body recover from the exertions of combat and running between towns. He felt depleted, for good reason.

A girl approached them. "Please—my father is in bad pain. Can you bite him too?"

"I can," Virtue said. There was no other answer she could give. Other women took note.

Before long Virtue had bitten a dozen injured men, and they were sleeping painlessly. Benny slept himself, knowing that she would rejoin him when she could.

In the morning, Bum had turned the corner. He would survive, but he would not be fully recovered for several more days.

"We will see to him," a woman told Virtue. "We have news from Elim, how he fought for them. We also appreciate what you have done for us. He will be safe here." Indeed, a buxom girl was holding the orc's head against her bosom as she spoon fed him gruel. Bum looked about as comfortable as a badly injured man could be.

"Then we must go," Benny said. He was feeling better after his night's rest.

Virtue kissed him, changed to bat form, bit him, and perched on his shoulder. They were on their way at inhuman speed.

Chapter 17

Gant was in shambles. Dead Kudgel warriors and village militia lay everywhere. Benny was shocked to see that some of the Kudgels were human, dwarf, and elf converts, a few of whom had lived in Gant and the surrounding area.

"How can they betray their own people?" he asked, appalled.

"It may not have been voluntary," Virtue said. "The Kudgels could have threatened their families, and spared them only if they joined their cause. Just as I joined yours."

Benny had no reply. His folk had slaughtered her folk, and only her commitment to him had saved her life. This was indeed how the real world operated, at times, ugly as it was. It just looked different when the enemy did it. Yet she had forgiven him.

"I always knew it wasn't your choice," she said, reading his mind. "You were innocent."

"Not anymore," he said, thinking of the killing he had done so recently.

"Neither am I. I helped you do your violence. We both have had to do what we had to do."

She was so supportive. "Oh, Virtue! Without you I'd

be nothing at all."

"I need you as much as you need me."

He wanted to pause in place and madly kiss her, but this was hardly the occasion, with bodies all around. Damn.

Mentally, she thought, and he felt the phantom pressure of her lips on his.

It would do.

Then they came upon Liverwart. The giant was sitting on the ground, injured, but not seriously. He was crying and holding the dead body of Nap, the halfling bard and poet who so often had serenaded the customers at the inn.

Suddenly, any remorse Benny might have suffered for the killing of Kudgels dissipated. This was what they were doing when not stopped.

But there was guilt. They had sent the giant home alone, as it were. Had they accompanied him, they might have been able to save Nap.

And we might have gotten killed ourselves, Virtue thought.

They would never know. They were limited to what they could do after the fact.

Benny stood beside Liverwart. "We share your grief," he said. "But there is another way to look at it. Nap is now in heaven with your family, who are surely welcoming him. He is with the Protector. He will be serenading his friends there."

The giant looked at him, hope dawning. "You think?"

"He's certainly not in hell."

Liverwart nodded, appreciating the reasoning.

Virtue bit the giant, temporarily relieving him of much of his grief. "Now you must bury him," she said. "In the town cemetery."

He stood, carrying Nap. "Bury with friends," he agreed,

partway cheered.

"We must go to the Fox Den," Benny said. "That's where Dale should be, defending it."

"Yes."

Then he paused. *Bide a while.*

He glanced at Virtue. "Did you just thought me?"

"No. I heard it too. It felt like the Protector."

"Why would he tell us to delay?"

"I don't know. But it felt troubled."

"How could the Protector be troubled? Isn't he all-powerful?"

"It must be complicated. Like a game where there remain no really good moves."

"Well, far be it from me to go against his wish." Benny enfolded Virtue, soundly kissing her.

She laughed with her mouth closed by his kiss. *I like the way you bide.*

But this was curious. What did it matter whether they arrived one moment or another? And why should it be troubling to the Protector?

In due course they resumed motion and followed the trail of dead bodies to the Fox Den. There was Helena sitting on the steps, covered in blood. For a moment Benny thought she was dead, but Virtue reassured him. "She's alive; that's the blood of her enemies on her naked body."

The Amazon heard her and looked up. "I'm glad you survived. Dale is inside. He's in a bad way. I have to leave him alone."

What did this mean?

"It's complicated," Virtue murmured.

It must be. Too bad this wasn't a mere game, where life and death were not an issue.

They entered the inn. There was a dead man on the floor. Benny realized in a moment that he was Red Rat Flack, the evil man whose blood had poisoned Virtue. His hood had been removed to reveal his horribly mutilated face. Layers of skin had been peeled off and healed over with crude grafts. What kind of a history had this bad man had?

Dale was sitting under the rainbow gnome fresco, crying. That brought Benny up short. Dale was not normally a man to show much emotion, least of all tears, and they couldn't be for a villain like Flack. What was going on?

"It's painful," Virtue whispered, and faded back. She of course had no grief for Flack, yet she did not seem relieved by his death.

Dale saw Benny. "I have done wrong. My conversion to the side of good can't fix this."

"I—I don't understand." That was the understatement of the day.

"I caught Flack. We fought and I killed him. Then he killed my soul."

Benny was silent, making too little sense of it to comment.

"As he lay dying," Dale continued, "Flack revealed himself to me. He is Dak Flack, the only surviving child from the orphans I killed at Alsbury. If I had known who he was, I'd have let him kill me."

Flack was one of the orphans? Benny's mind groped for sense without getting any good hold on it.

"A few of the orcs who weren't killed by the villagers of Alsbury fled with his dying body, into the western deserts, and were taken in by Kudgels. They healed him, and he plotted with them to take revenge on the world that had let him get hurt."

"Revenge?"

"It is understandable. I would feel the same in a similar situation."

Benny thought of his own reaction to the murder of his friends, and had to agree. But the matter remained curious. For one thing, it was clear that however justified Flack's pain was, he had gone on to inflict similar pain on those innocent of any crime with respect to him. Misery had not ennobled him.

"Flack was not the leader of the Kudgels," Dale continued. "But he told me the real leader was someone very close to me. Then he died before he could say more." He made as if to pull out handfuls of his own hair. "But that was more than enough to show me how much I wronged him."

There really was little positive to be said at this point, so Benny focused on the practical. He searched Flack's body and found a note. He read it.

MEET ME AT A RUINED FORTRESS IN THE FOREST OUTSIDE DAN, TO GO OVER BATTLE PLANS. At the bottom was the symbol of the Grand Exalted Cyclops.

Benny felt a chill. The Cyclops had been tormenting him for years. Now they had the spelled witch hazel to fend it off, but hadn't used it. That reminded him of the mystery: why was the Cyclops after him? He still had no idea.

A crazy idea flickered through his mind. Could he pretend to be Flack and meet with the Cyclops? No; the Cyclops could get into his mind and would know. Still, this did give them a way to locate the Cyclops, whoever he was.

Benny left Dale to his torment and walked out of the inn. Virtue followed. "I will skry it," she said.

She did, and learned that the author of the note was

indeed the High Exalted Cyclops, the true secret leader of the Kudgels.

Dale emerged from the inn, his grief spent for the moment.

"Where is Laughing Jack?" Benny asked, avoiding the subject of Flack.

"I lost track of him during the fight."

They searched the premises and soon found Jack in his bedroom, dying. A Kudgel sword was sticking out of his gut. The Kudgel warrior was dead; Jack had given a fair account of himself.

"Oh, no!" Benny cried, and Virtue went to try to help the man.

"Too late for that, dear girl," Jack wheezed. "I am done for."

She assessed him, mentally as well as physically, and nodded. "True. But I can ease your pain."

"Do that, for I have something to say."

Virtue bit him, and he relaxed.

"We should have been here sooner," Benny said. "We might have stopped the Kudgels."

"Yes, you might have," Jack said, speaking more clearly now. "I acted to prevent that."

They stared at him, not comprehending.

Dale appeared. "Damn! I should not have left you alone!"

"Cease the recriminations," Jack said. "Here is the story. I was hiding in my room when the Kudgels came. I overheard them talking. They knew of a prophecy that two who should live would die here today. I had heard that prophecy before, and forgotten it, but now I knew that it was true. It could not be avoided. Two would die. They knew that

Benny and Virtue were returning. So they set an ambush, to kill the two of you when you entered the inn, fulfilling the prophecy to their advantage." He smiled, briefly. "For some reason they have had trouble taking you two out. Maybe it relates in some devious way to the mind reading of the one, and the spot ghosting of the other. But buttressed by the prophecy, they were sure they could succeed this time. I feared they were right."

Benny opened his mouth, but Jack silenced him with a gesture. "Please do not interrupt me. Virtue's bite will not last long, and then the pain will return to shut my mouth. Just let me speak."

Benny closed his mouth.

"I knew I did not want you dear friends to die. Fortunately the prophecy did not say who would die, just that they were ones who should live. I knew I qualified for that, and I hoped there was another in the inn. At any rate, I could save at least one of you. So when their snare was laid, I burst upon them and managed to take out one Kudgel. But the other got me before I dispatched him, and here I am. Congratulations on your survival, whichever one of you I managed to save. Probably Benny."

"I saved the other," Dale said. "By killing one I would have spared. So maybe I saved Virtue. If it had to be Flack's life or hers, I would always choose hers, much as I hated the choice."

There were no good moves left in this game.

"Had you come sooner, it might well have been otherwise," Jack said.

Dale nodded. "So there was reason for their delay."

"There was reason," Jack agreed.

Now Benny spoke. "We received a—a message.

Telling us to delay briefly. So we did, not realizing what was happening here. Had we known--"

"Which is why you were prevented from knowing," Jack said. "You have things yet to do in life, while mine was largely finished anyway. So it was right that it be this way. Now farewell; I trust I go to a better place."

Benny, Virtue, and Dale closed in to embrace him together. Then Jack closed his eyes and died, smiling.

"He surely is going to a better place," Benny agreed. "I don't think the Protector would have let him go, otherwise."

"And we had better see that we do right by *this* place," Dale said. "Considering his sacrifice. We still have work to do here."

Benny could only agree.

Chapter 18

That night, after dark, Dale, Helena, Benny, and Virtue set out for the fortress ruins to rendezvous and with luck kill the leader of the Kudgels. It would have been better to travel by day, but they wanted to surprise the enemy, both in timing and by being in the cover of darkness. Benny might have preferred to leave Virtue in Gant, for her safety, but she wouldn't have it, for *his* safety. How could he deny her? He hated being apart from her anyway.

They used night lights, which cast no glow but enabled them to see well enough to place their feet. Progress was slow, but before dawn they were in the forest near the fortress just beyond the border of Dan.

Virtue did a skry to ascertain the best time to attack. "Not for two hours yet," she said.

"Then we shall rest," Dale said. He and Helena lay down under some thick brush and were soon asleep. Benny and Virtue did the same, under a blanket beside a boulder. Virtue laid her hand on his forehead, and touched him with her mind, and he was in slumber too.

In an hour he woke, Virtue sleeping beside him in the pre-dawn gloom. He had a call of nature, so he quietly got up, got beyond odor range, and sought a suitable crevice to use. Then he stood and started back.

"Hello." Benny jumped; it was Helena, whom he recognized more by her voice than her shadowed appearance. What was she doing here?

Oh. The same thing he was doing, of course. "Uh, hello," he said, embarrassed. Natural functions were not discussed in mixed company.

He made as if to pass her, but she blocked him off. "Why the hurry?" she asked.

"I—I am done here."

Still she barred his way. "There is time."

"Time for what?"

"I think you know."

He didn't know, but he had an ugly suspicion. "Did you follow me here?"

"Do not return yet to the vampire."

It seemed impossible that she had any social interest in him. She could not be looking for any dalliance. So what was she up to? "Helena--"

She put her hands on his arms, holding him in place. "Did you like my kiss, before?"

That set him back. He *had* liked the kiss, surprisingly, which had amused Virtue as she read his mind. "That means nothing. I would never--"

She cut him off with a new kiss. He hated that he liked it again.

She drew her face back slightly. "We can do it here. It is expedient. Dale and Virtue need never know."

Guilt buffeted him for even thinking about it. "Helena--"

"We don't need to lie down. Amazons are adept at

awkward positions." Her hands moved to his shirt as if to unbutton it.

Something erupted in him. It felt like utter fury. *Enough of this nonsense! Time is running out.*

"Well, hello, Cyclops!" Helena said brightly, recognizing the change. "Did you crave a kiss too?"

She was right. The Cyclops had just taken over his body. Always before it had struck during his sleep, horrifying and terrifying him. This time it had taken full possession, and mayhem was its urge. Benny wanted to speak, to warn her, but he no longer had power over his own body.

"Get clear, Amazon trash," his mouth said. "You're a secondary target at the moment."

"And you had to get your prospective host away from your primary target," Helena said, "lest she interfere, as she has before."

"Yes. Some distance was necessary, to mute her telepathic awareness, even in sleep. Now let go."

Her arms tightened around his body, holding him helpless with her Amazon strength. "Make me."

His body made an incoherent growl as it struggled to free his arms so he could grab a weapon. But she held him in a bear hug. In fact she was heaving him up off the ground. Benny had forgotten how strong she was, as maybe had the Cyclops.

"And exactly who is your primary target, sweet stuff?" she asked teasingly. They had just covered this; why was she repeating it?

"The vampire, of course! With her telepathy and her bites and the way she holds this host in thrall. She has to go."

The Cyclops wanted to kill Virtue? Using Benny's body? His horror magnified. Benny struggled with renewed determination, but still could not break the deadly mental hold on him. Any more than the Cyclops could break the Amazon's physical hold on him.

"And that's why your nocturnal campaigns against Benny," Helena said. "Gradually breaking down his spirit, so you could take over his body and use it to betray his own side at a critical moment."

Suddenly, those awful sieges made sense! Helena was making sure he understood, now that it was too late.

"Yes, you tattooed slut! Now let go before I hurt you."

Helena smiled broadly, while tightening her hold. "Hurt me, turd heart."

Rage overcame the Cyclops. The head shot forward, and the mouth bit the Amazon's cheek, hard. Blood appeared.

"Is that the best you can do, green eyeball?" she asked, laughing.

The Cyclops spat out the blood and launched again, biting her left ear, tearing at it like a feeding wolf.

Then the Cyclops froze. "Damnation! Curse you, she-wolf!"

She smiled despite her wounds. "I stand accursed, sucker."

And the Cyclops faded out. Benny was free.

"It's me," he gasped. "Please, Helena--"

She let him go. "Now you know why I shadowed you."

"Now I know," he agreed. "To stop the Cyclops. How did you do it?"

"I gave him a taste of my blood. Remember, it is effective against alien possession, once imbibed. He could not remain thereafter."

Benny was amazed and gratified. Helena had tricked the Cyclops into biting her, so as to deliver the blood. "But how did you know the Cyclops was coming?"

"I am a warrior. That includes strategy. The worst thing you can do to an enemy is plant a traitor in his midst, to strike at the critical moment, such as amid a battle, when he least expects it. You told us how the Cyclops was stalking you. I suspected that the Kudgels were trying to make you that traitor, by gradually breaking down your willpower until at a moment of highest tension you would be vulnerable. But I also suspected that they couldn't do it as long as you were buttressed by Virtue. So they had to take her out first. I had to be close enough to intercept that. I owe Virtue too much to let her get hurt like that."

"Oh, Helena, may I kiss you for real?"

She laughed. "Yes, now."

He kissed her, getting blood on his face. "Oh. I smeared you."

She produced a cloth and wiped her cheek and ear, only now thinking of her injuries. "Sorry about that." Then she wiped her blood off his face, too, and his bloodstained teeth.

He laughed weakly. "I thought you were coming on to me."

"I had to make the Cyclops think that. So he'd figure it'd be forever before he got to go after Virtue. He just couldn't wait; he had to kill her while she remained asleep, because the moment she woke she'd read his mind and drive him out. Timing was critical. Folk do get careless when impatient." She smiled. "No offense, Benny; I owe you a lot, but you're not my type."

He smiled back. "Knowing what you were up to, making out with you would almost be worth it. No offense."

They both laughed. Then they returned to the others. Both Dale and Virtue were up, now, missing them in the dim coming light of the day. "Your face!" Dale said, seeing the damage to Helena.

She laughed. "Benny kissed me. Maybe he was a bit clumsy, even for him."

"Mere love bites," Benny said, looking at her torn ear.

There was a moment of frozen silence. Then Virtue read their minds, and laughed too. She hugged Helena. That gave Dale a clue.

Benny quickly caught them up on what had happened. "Now they know we know," Virtue said. "Time for the spelled witch hazel." She produced a jar from somewhere and rubbed it on his face and into his hair. The Cyclops could neither attack him nor spy on him anymore.

"Give me some of that," Helena said. She dabbed it on her wounds, and they did seem to fade. It was marvelous stuff.

Now it was dawn. Time to make their move, according to Virtue's skry. "There are not many Kudgels here," she said. "This is a private command post, not the main enemy camp. Most of the troops and their allies are out raiding the towns. So there's not much traffic here. But there are some, and it seems they know we're coming."

"Obviously so," Dale agreed. "The Cyclops hoped to have things under control, taking over Benny to replace Flack and killing the rest of us by that treachery before we even got here." He glanced at Helena. "Which you stopped. Remind me some time to tell you why I love you."

"I will. Just don't kiss me the way Benny did."

"But you do look good enough to eat."

"I can make you seem a bit fuzzy," Virtue said, "by telepathically clouding their minds. You will have an advantage."

"Just you be invisible to them," Benny said. "Now that we know how badly they want to kill you."

"Invisible," she agreed.

"Here's the plan," Helena said, shaking her head no. Benny realized that the Kudgels could still be spying on them, by listening in, so this was for their benefit. "There are only three of us fighting, and maybe a dozen of them, so we need to stay together and guard each other's backs. We can sneak behind that big tree by the gate, then charge from there, catching them by surprise. Got it?"

"Got it," Dale and Benny said almost together.

Helena closed her mouth and signaled to Benny.

Benny took over. He pointed to Dale, then to the right: go that way. Then he pointed to Helena, and to the left: that way. Then himself, and straight ahead toward the tree. Virtue would be with him, alerting him to enemy presence while fuzzing the enemy minds. They could come together again soon enough, inside the compound.

Now Dale did kiss Helena, and Benny kissed Virtue. They all knew that this was extremely dangerous, and one or all of them could die. With luck they would take out the Cyclops, either way, and that would disrupt the Kudgel invasion. It had to be done.

They separated, going their ways. Benny crept up on the tree Helena had identified. Of course, the Kudgels would be massed there. Benny was a distraction so that Dale and Helena could safely enter the fortress. He just hoped that Virtue's mental fuzzing messed up their focus.

They are there, her thought came. *Six of them. Now I will bite you.*

She bit him, and he felt the berserker mode coming on. He activated his club, which Dale had let him keep for now. That was best for this, because it was less likely to get snagged on enemy flesh and slow the action.

Benny stepped around the tree. There were the Kudgels, rising from their hiding places behind bushes. Benny waded in, swinging the club.

Two warriors closed in on him, the others behind, because there was not room for any more. They had evidently expected him to back up against the trunk of the tree, for cover, but he remained in the open, for effect. He smashed one head, then the other, and the two went down. His reflexes were faster than theirs, in this mode.

Two more charged him, swinging their swords wildly, as if they did not know his precise position, thanks to Virtue's fuzzing. He clubbed their knees, dropping them in screaming pain.

The last two came, better coordinated. One attacked high, the other low. This was deadly, as Benny knew from prior experience. He clipped the legs out from under one, but the other scored on his head. Without effect, as he ghosted at the key moment. Then he bashed that one's head as he swung about, for the moment vulnerable.

Six Kudgels were dead or down for the duration. Benny moved on.

Only to encounter something worse: a mountain giant garbed in a green robe. Not only was the man huge and strong, he had magic; Benny felt it buffeting him, setting him back. He would not be able to ghost clear of this one's strike.

"Who are you?" Benny demanded, stalling for time.

Bad guys loved to brag; it seemed to be an article of their faith. "I am the Grand Hydra," the giant said. "I will destroy you and your puny magic." He raised his huge sword.

This was mischief. Benny would have to dodge quickly

enough to avoid the strike, hoping he would get an opening for a counter-strike.

"Ho, varlet!" It was Dale, coming in from the right side.

"Defend yourself, meat face!" It was Helena, appearing to the left side.

Suddenly the odds had evened. The giant gazed at them. "Oh, beans!" he swore. "This is more trouble than it's worth." He stomped off.

They looked at each other. *He learned he was not supposed to kill Benny,* Virtue's thought came. *So he quit in disgust.*

"Why am I not supposed to be killed?" Benny asked.

"The Cyclops wants to use you alive," Helena said. "That's why he's been after you all along."

"I'd rather be kissing you," Benny said.

They laughed. Then they moved cautiously on into the fortress. It was deserted; evidently they had gotten rid of all its defendants. But where was the Grand Exalted Cyclops?

They discovered one solid part of the ruins that must have been restored. They entered, alert for traps or ambush, but all remained quiet. Virtue's telepathic awareness did not indicate any immediate threats. The interior was clean, with food neatly stored and insulating carpets on the walls and floor. There were even books on bookshelves, in the manner of a library. In this context it was distinctly weird.

And there was the secret leader, seated at a desk, reading from an ancient-looking tome by candlelight, like any other scholar. He wore a black robe with the great green eye of the High Exalted Cyclops on the front.

Benny felt a chill. This was the man who had been mentally persecuting him?

They halted before the desk. Virtue appeared. "He knows who we are, but I can't read his mind to know who he is."

"And I can't tell you," Helena said. "But soon it will be clear. Very soon."

"Yes, I knew you were coming," the robed man said. "I set a token defense so you would be sure to get here on schedule. The roots of the Kudgel army run so thick that you will never get out of here, let alone defeat them all. But for the moment we are free to talk. I give you this one, last chance: join us, and become privileged officers in the new order. You, each of you, have talents we can use." He paused as if smiling in the deep shadow of his hood. "Especially the winsome vampire lass."

"You are disgusting," Virtue snapped.

"I was referring to your mind reading and your evocative bites, both singularly useful to a leader," the Cyclops said with another seeming smile. "The Amazon will do for erotic purposes, especially since she is not pregnant or in her blood cycle at the moment."

"Try it, and I'll cut your dinky member off and feed it to you," Helena said. "I know who you are."

The man ignored that. "Dale Beranger is an excellent warrior."

"Not for your team," Dale said. "I serve the cause of good, not evil."

"And Benny Clout, with the lovely ghosting ability. That is perhaps the most desirable, as I have not encountered it elsewhere."

"Well, desire this," Benny said, showing one finger.

"I take it that the four of you are declining my generous offer."

"And there you are correct," Dale said. "Now will you submit peacefully to arrest and trial, or will we have to kill you first?"

"None of the above." The Cyclops stood and threw off his robe and hood to reveal--

"Purp!" Dale said, shocked. "My head butler!"

Benny and Virtue stared, almost beyond words, similarly recognizing the man. It was the purple servant who had seen to the operation of the mansion in Upper Sultry, except that now his eyes were the same shade of green as in his Cyclops nightmares.

"I do have to admire the way you went openly among us," Helena said. "I knew I didn't like you, but didn't know why, until I learned your identity. You were right there in the mansion all the time."

"It was a convenient hiding place," Purp agreed. "Ideal for tuning in on news of the planet." Then, taking advantage of their stasis, he lifted his hand and fired a fireball spell at Dale.

But Benny was already in motion. He lurched into Dale, knocking him out of the way, and took the blast himself. He stifled his ghost response, wanting to protect his friend. He was holding the club, and it deflected the fire as it melted, but the heat still scorched him painfully.

Helena leaped forward, her sword stabbing at Purp's chest. But he moved his fingers, and a levitation spell lifted her into the air and threw her into a wall. Reacting quickly, she twisted her body so as to strike the wall with her feet, avoiding injury. But she was out of position, leaving only Dale before Purp.

Dale did not try to attack. "Why did you join the Kudgels?" he asked.

And Purp answered. "I was sick of being treated like an outcast. I joined because I felt that nobody else loved and cared for me. I was apt, and quickly rose through their ranks to their top office. I studied magic along the way, which helped. I wanted to take revenge on the cruel world. Now I am doing that."

"But I really cared for you, and still do," Dale said. "That's why I kept you as my most trusted servant."

"And I cared for you," Purp replied. "And still do. You were the only person who ever showed me respect or compassion, and I thank you for that. But this is war."

"Renounce your evil ways. There is still time."

"And why should I do a thing like that?"

"Because I did. I struggled with my evil side, and was losing, until Virtue enabled my good side to prevail. She can do the same for you."

"No. What I am doing is good, and everything else is evil. It is you who are doing evil now, serving the wrong side. I'm simply repaying those who wronged me."

Dale shook his head. "You are hopelessly reversed."

"That is as you see it. But I am also a very powerful sorcerer. You are doomed."

Benny and Dale leaped forward, but Purp's fingers turned into long tentacles that wrapped around them both and began choking them to death. Benny remembered those tentacles from his nightmares. Purp was not fooling about his sorcery! They were helpless.

Helena attacked again, this time more than physically. She scraped her fingers across her own damaged ear and flung the blood at Purp. He winced and cast a deflection shield so as to avoid the spray. That was successful, with only a single small drop striking one tentacle, where it smoldered. But his concentration was weakened and Dale and Benny twisted free of his grasp as his tentacles faded back into fingers.

Dale hit Purp on the head with the butt end of his sword, but the Cyclops managed to grab the weapon. Dale wrenched it back, but Purp drew his own sword and attacked. Now it was sword against sword, and in moment it was apparent that Purp was the better swordsman.

Benny and Helena drew their swords and attacked, but Purp was so skilled that he beat back all three. Dale went into berserk mode, but Purp then sprouted an extra set of armored arms and was still overpowering the trio. No wonder he hadn't feared them! Physically and magically he was more than their match.

Then Purp stabbed Benny in the chest. Benny's ghosting avoided it, which surprised him, because the Cyclops could nullify his magic and he had already been weakened by the fireball.

"I knew your talent would accommodate it," Purp said. "I am saving you for later use. This is just to remind you that your life is hostage to my convenience."

"Never!"

"Oh, you will cooperate when I start torturing your vamp wife."

That froze Benny. It seemed that the Cyclops could and would do that to gain his ends, and Benny knew he would not be able to let it happen.

But that momentary diversion of the Cyclops' attention allowed Dale to use his Mage cry to blast Purp with lightning. That rocked him back, surprised, and gave them a key advantage. The need to brag had weakened him, just as it had the green mountain giant. They followed up without mercy, knowing that any break in the action could be disastrous, and soon the man was on the floor, unconscious.

Benny, still angry about the way Laughing Jack had died, and by the threat to Virtue, raised his sword to hack off the Cyclops' head.

"Wait!" Dale said, making Benny pause. "Remember the mercy you and Virtue showed me. Can you do less for him?"

"He's right," Helena said. "We should tie him up, spellbind him, and carry him back to Gant for questioning. We still need to learn what we can of the Kudgels' future plans, so we can counter them."

Virtue appeared, nodding agreement. True to her nature, she responded to the threat of torture with forgiveness.

Benny sighed. They were right. Sometimes mercy made sense tactically as well as morally.

CHAPTER 19

They found a wagon with a horse in a nearby stable, evidently one the Cyclops used for traveling, and used it to cart their captive along forest trails toward Gant. Virtue did a skry on the appropriate route.

"That's an odd choice," she said. "But I trust its magic. We'll use that trail."

No one argued about the details of individual routes. They just wanted to get this done.

They boarded the wagon, guarding the unconscious man. Benny sat up front and guided the horse. Helena sat beside him, as Virtue was keeping a close eye and mind on Purp. It was easy for Benny and Helena to talk with the two immediately behind them.

Purp woke. "You're too late for information," he said. "I have taken a lethal potion and will die within the hour. There is no antidote."

"You're bluffing," Helena said, glancing back. "We stripped your body of all devices, and you know we will cut off your tentacles if you try to grow them."

"Ask the vamp, sweetie. My mind is open."

"Oh!" Virtue said. "He had it in a hollow tooth. We

didn't think of that."

Helena banged her forehead with the heel of her hand as if knocking out the dottle from an empty pipe. "Standard ploy! What were we thinking?"

"You were so busy nullifying my magic you never thought of garden variety poison. An elementary error, warrior girl." The Cyclops' contempt was obvious.

"But why?" Dale asked. "We spared your life so we could question you, then maybe convert you to the side of good, as I was converted. That is no bad thing."

"It is a fate worse than death. I would rather die than be a part of the world that scorned me."

"Oh, Purp, forgive me for not making you feel more appreciated," Dale said sincerely. "I always respected you, despite not knowing your larger mission."

"I was never angry with you personally. I would have spared you from the Kudgel conquest and left you to live peacefully in your mansion, if you hadn't gotten involved in the war. I didn't know about Flack's revenge until later, and figured you could handle that yourself."

"Please, I beg you, tell us about the Kudgels' plans," Dale said. "There's a tremendous amount of pain and sorrow you can prevent."

"What do I care about the pain of the world? It didn't care about mine."

"But there is one who does care," Helena said, glancing back again. "You should do it for her."

"Who? The vampire?" Purp demanded dismissively. "She'd care for the hurt feelings of a scorpion."

Virtue nodded, agreeing. Benny felt it in her mind.

"Your sister," Helena said. "Magenta."

"Magenta! She fled from me and became a whore."

"She fled because she loved you and could not betray you, but neither could she tolerate the destruction you planned to unleash on the world," Helena said evenly. "She earned her living the only way she could without attracting attention, hidden in the slum so that no one would think to use her against you. That is what you did to her. She is a good person, enduring a life of humiliation in her effort to do the right thing. But she will die in the Kudgel conquest, after being gang raped, because she is a beautiful woman; you know that."

"I know that," Purp said brokenly. "I do love her, and would spare her if I could. I would do anything for her, now that I know what she did for me. But it's too late. I am dying, and she is far away."

"Far away physically," Helena said. "But perhaps not mentally. Will you talk to her, if she comes telepathically?"

"Yes! Let me be with her before I die." The discussion of his sister had made him into a completely different man. It seemed that whatever good there was in him was connected to his memory of Magenta.

Helena glanced back at Virtue. "Signal Tele, who I know is not far distant. Bring him here."

"We are already on the way to him," Virtue said. "I skried our route, and that put us in that direction. I did not know why, until this moment."

"Good girl," Helena said. "Now we will need a temporary local host, so Magenta can actually touch her brother. I don't think you will do for this, vampire; we'll need you to complete the telepathic linkage, as before. So, by elimination..." She did not finish.

"What, you can't host a whore?" Dale asked, laughing.

"I can host a good person. That's not the problem."

"What a nuisance," Purp complained. "I can't kiss my sister without kissing you, blooded Amazon? Maybe I'll be lucky enough to die first."

"No. That would make it pointless. But I'm hardly keen on it myself. *That* is the problem." Helena sighed. "But it is expedient. I promised to be there for her when she needed me. That time is now. I will do what I have to do, as an Amazon does."

Benny remembered again how Helena had honored her deal with him by saving Virtue. Now she was doing something similar with Magenta.

They were approaching Tele's residence. Benny drew the horse and wagon to a halt.

Tele emerged. "Virtue minded me," he said. "There is little time. I will join you there." He climbed onto the wagon. "Ready, Virtue?"

"Ready," Virtue agreed.

Then Helena changed. She seemed to shrink to a more petite form, and her scars and tattoos faded. Her skin turned green, her face and hair purple, with bright green eyes. Her rough battle clothing metamorphosed into the exposing gown of a prostitute. In fact she looked like Magenta, and she was surpassingly lovely in a delicate feminine way; it was an amazing transformation. Benny knew it was illusion clothing the physical woman, but it was extraordinarily realistic.

"Hello, all," Magenta said, soft voiced. "I am glad to meet you again. But what is the occasion?"

"Magenta!" Purp exclaimed.

"Snus!" she exclaimed in return, knowing his real name rather than the one Dale had given him. "I can't be with you!"

"Yes, you can," Benny said. "He is dying, and wanted

to see you before he departed. You can do him no harm now, but you can comfort him, if you wish to."

"Oh, I do, I do!" She dropped down beside Purp, stroking his face with her hands. "Oh, my brother, I never wished this upon you!"

"Nor I this on you, my sister," he replied. "But I wanted to kiss you one last time, and beg your forgiveness."

"Oh, you have it! I always wanted only the best for you, my brother, though I could not share it." She kissed him avidly on the mouth.

"Then I can die relieved," Purp said. "I thank you for coming."

"Not yet," Benny said, because at this moment Helena could not speak for herself.

"Not?" Magenta asked. "But I feel the death closing on his heart."

"Purp," Benny said. "Or Snus, or Cyclops, whatever. The raping and killing. Only you can save her. You know how."

"What do you mean?" Magenta asked. It was evident that she had none of the memories of her host.

Purp shuddered. "When the Kudgels I have unleashed conquer the cities, they will abuse the citizens before killing them. It is part of their vengeance against the old order. I am appalled in retrospect; I am suffering great remorse. I do not want this for you, my beloved sibling."

Magenta laughed without humor. "You forget my profession. I cannot be abused."

"You do not know the Kudgels of my army. They enjoy making lovely women scream in agony. That is what turns them on." He paused. It was evident that he was growing weaker. "This must be stopped. You must stop them, for your sake and the sake of all other women."

"How could I ever do that?"

"You must take over from me. You must lead them to peace and decency."

"I can't do any such thing! I know nothing of armies."

"Yes, you can. In fact, only you can do it, because you are my closest kin; my body and brain will yield their secrets to you. Kiss me again, as I die. Take the information from my mind. You will have it all, and with the help of your friends here, you will be able to do it."

"Oh, Snus! I would far rather save your life!"

"That you can't do. But you can save my soul. Now, please, before I fade."

Tearfully, Magenta yielded. She bent down and kissed him again, deeply. Her body shuddered, as did his. There was a momentary glow.

Then she raised her head. Green tears streaked her purple face. "Rest in peace, my brother," she said. "I will do what you wish."

It was clear that Purp was dead. Yet his expression was one of peace.

Now Magenta addressed the others. "I have his information. I know the battle strategies. I know the names, locations, and assignments of all his troops. I will command them, and the conquest will be turned aside. There will be no rapine. But this is complicated; there will have to be many orders, correctly phrased; an army does not turn on a pinhead. I will have to return to my own body and get in touch with you as myself. In the interim, I ask you to see to the disposition of his body; I regret I can't attend."

"We will do that," Benny said.

"We will," Dale agreed.

Magenta smiled, and her beauty radiated like a flaring torch. "I know you will. You are good men. I wish I could do more for you, in the way that I am practiced. But I suspect that my host would object, not to mention your women."

They laughed. It had to be a joke.

"Oh, one more item before I go. There is one thing you must attend to immediately. A huge battalion of Kudgels will be heading for the Northern Mountains, to blow the horn which will summon the Sky Titans. This is what the Kudgels were to do if my brother was somehow killed or defeated in battle. They will soon know he is gone, and will act. They must be stopped; the Titans will bring utter devastation to the land. The Kudgels don't care about their own survival. They just want the world to burn. Do not let that horn be blown!"

Then she faded, and Helena returned. "I was listening. She's not fooling. We have another job to do."

"She's not fooling," Virtue agreed.

"We were getting bored by the inaction anyway," Dale joked.

"I leave you to your campaign," Tele said, climbing off the wagon.

"But we have to bury the body," Benny said. "We can't just leave it exposed. It was the only thing she asked of us, for her brother."

"I don't think we can wait for that," Helena said. "Magenta absorbed a lot of information in a hurry, and still has to assimilate most of it, which I think she will by the time we can get together with her physically. I really have only a passing sniff of it. But that horn is paramount; we have to get on it immediately. That much I know."

Benny looked at them, then at the body. A proper burial

would take hours, because of the attendant ceremony. But it would not be proper to leave the body to rot while they headed for the mountains. What could they do?

Then the body shimmered. Was Purp coming back to life? It glowed, becoming fire-bright. Then it disappeared.

"He's a wizard," Dale said. "Can he raise himself from the dead?"

"That did not look like it," Helena said. "That looked like an impromptu fire burial."

"There was no mind manifesting," Virtue said. "He did not come alive."

"I think we have had a sign from above," Benny said. "We are relieved of the chore of burial. The Protector has taken care of it directly."

Dale nodded. "I think we are relieved. Now all we have to do is stop that horn from getting blown. Why do I suspect that will not be easy?"

"You have a suspicious mind," Helena chided him. "As do I. Now stop dawdling and get to work."

Benny resumed guiding the horse. They had to get to Gant, then figure out how to tackle the horn. Soon. Indeed, it promised to be a challenge. But if the matter were so urgent that the Protector needed to intervene to enable it, they certainly had to take it seriously.

Now Virtue joined him up front. "We do," she agreed.

But at least he had her beside him.

"Always," she said, smiling.

EPILOGUE

The boy had fallen asleep towards the end of the story, around the same time as the Pawben was describing the death of Red Rat Flack. It was probably a good thing the boy didn't hear the rest. The boy wouldn't remember a tenth of the story by the next day, and the Pawben had been rambling on for most of the day. His throat was dry, his stomach was empty and he didn't feel like making the trek back to his cottage.

"Y'all can stay the night if you want. I'll make some stew for supper." Toadstool stood up and walked to the kitchen.

"The boy's been pestering me forever and when I finally tell the story, he passes out." The old man laughed.

"To him it's just a story."

"Sometimes I wish that's all it ever was..." Pawben stared into the middle distance.

"When are you gonna tell him, Ben?"

Pawben was stirred by the mentioning of his real name. "Shhh! I don't know. I guess I'll have to tell him eventually, when he starts asking questions about his folks and whatnot. Frankly, I wouldn't mind if I never told him at all. Sometimes, I wish Pakk never existed."

"Oh, come on Ben. After all that talk about teamwork, mercy and forgiveness? What turned you so sour on your homeland? Those Sky Titans must've really done a number on you."

"No, it wasn't them…it's what happened long after that."

"Well, no world is perfect, not even Gold Mulch Wood. Pakk can't be that bad." Toadstool began pouring contents into a large pot on his stove.

"I'm almost two hundred and fourteen years old, and have spent many years in dozens of worlds and dimensions. But to this day, none were as terrible as Pakk was to become. Sure, I helped win Dale to the good side, we defeated the Kudgel uprising, survived the wrath of the Sky Titans, and more. But eventually everything has to go sour."

Toadstool attempted to change the subject. "You're that old? But if the lad is Dale's grandson, that's not even feasible."

"Time works differently in different worlds. I once spent twenty years in one world, and upon returning to Pakk, I'd found only a few weeks had passed since my departure."

"I dare say if you wrote down all your adventures there wouldn't be enough room in the whole wood to contain their contents!"

"And you won't shut up until you make me tell you every one, will you?" Pawben grinned.

"You know it! But don't bother telling anymore today. Tomorrow we'll go for a picnic and you can tell us about the Sky Titans, and how you earned your nickname, Benny the Beast!"

A twinge shot through the Pawben's back when he

heard the nickname that would brand him for most of his life…the name that would bring about the death of his most dearly loved friends and family. Toadstool saw the look on the Pawben's face, and quickly tried to diffuse the old man's rage. "I'm sorry, Ben. I didn't realize…"

"…how much of an idiot you are?" Pawben winked to show there was no hostility. "I tell these stories because I'm trying to help others prevent and stay away from the things I fell into. The message of this story is to always treat living creatures, especially intelligent ones, with love, respect and dignity, regardless of race, skin color, gender, or past experience. No two people react to the same thing the same way. If you treat someone like a sub-human beast their entire life, how do you expect them to grow up to become anything more than that?"

"Kind of like the old saying, 'what goes around comes around?'" Toadstool asked.

"Something like that."

Pawben carried the boy up into Toadstool's bedroom and tucked him in along with Flack the rat, who had dozed off as well. Pawben and Toadstool stayed up into the late hours of the night, playing cards, telling jokes, and playing pranks on each other. For at least one night, Pawben, otherwise known as Benny Clout, Benny the Beast, Pa Ben, Wayne Pawben, and countless other names, felt as if he were sitting back at the Fox Den with Laughing Jack, Virtue, Dale, Helena and Bum. He could almost hear Nap's annoying yet beautiful singing in the background. Pawben still had some years left to live, but he was reassured by the thought of one day reuniting with his friends, wives, and children. Later that night, just before dozing off on the couch after playing dice with Toadstool, he heard the voice of the Protector speaking to him: *They miss you too, Benny. By the way, Jack and Dale think you should trim that scraggily beard.* Benny chuckled and fell asleep. It felt like Virtue was holding his head in her arms.

Author's Note: Piers Anthony

Amazon Expedient is the sequel to *Virtue Inverted*, and there is more to come. In the first episode we saw how a vampire turned out to be the nicest girl you'd want to meet; in this one we saw how a tattooed Amazon warrior woman made a real difference in the lives of ordinary folk in ways other than combat. Virtue is a vampire, and Helena is a warrior, but we value them for their other qualities, such as gentleness and expedience. It's not smart to judge anyone superficially. Who knows what we'll discover hereafter?

Between these books I turned 81, and no, I am not yet ready to humor the bucket that says KICK ME. I like mainly to write, but life can get in the way. The day before I settled down to address my collaborator Ken Kelly's work on *Amazon*, lightning struck our house. No, I don't think the Protector was trying to warn me off. But it did slow things somewhat. We lost our security alarm system—there were actually scorch marks on its panel— our phone—fortunately we have cell phones to fill in— our upstairs air conditioner— my working study is upstairs; in fact it sounded as if the thunderbolt was ten feet over my head, as it may have been—my computer modem, and assorted other devices. My wife and I—we've been married 59 years—had to sleep downstairs to avoid the stifling heat, with the complications that entailed. At least we didn't lose our electricity or water; it could have been worse. Overall, it cost us about $5,000 in repairs. I could not run the computer long, lest it overheat and degrade in the Florida summer, so it took me several days to catch up on Ken's material. I was also suffering through the dread Soft Diet, as I had all my upper teeth out, to be replaced with implants and a denture, and was amid a four month healing period. Throughout my life I have had little but trouble from my teeth, regardless how well I take care of them, so finally I'm getting rid of them. So I couldn't even grind my teeth when there were problems; there were no teeth to grind.

After a week, when things were mostly back to normal, I started writing, and Ken wrote, and I wrote, back and forth in the manner of the collaboration it is. It continued from there, and in October we had it written. We hope you like the result.

You can check me out further at my web site, www. HiPiers.com, where I run a monthly blog-type column, and an ongoing survey of electronic publishers and related services, intended to assist writers who need such information.

Amazon Expedient was proofread by Scott M Ryan and Anne White.

Kenneth Kelly's Author's Note

Virtue Inverted started as an unnamed, handwritten manuscript in my final year of high school; even then I'd had hopes of developing it into a series. After completing *Virtue* with Piers Anthony my mind began to race with ideas as I began to piece together an outline for its sequel, *Amazon Expedient.* Piers Anthony, who had inspired and helped me realize my calling as a writer, had been gracious enough to help me write the first book. But would he be willing to help me with further projects? If you're reading this author's note you already know the answer. The story itself – though not necessarily the overall plot structure – for *Amazon Expedient* was more complex than its prequel, with a greater number of characters, battles and places explored. It also introduces the name of the fantasy world both *Virtue* and *Amazon* are set in: Pakk. Could I have come up with something better? That's a stupid question. Of course, I could have! But, since Piers Anthony and I wrote these books together, I came up with an acronym made up of the initials of our pen names. We'll see what the readers think of it.

Like its prequel, *Amazon Expedient* contains religious themes, primarily through the character of the Protector (Search/God). However, I tried to portray messages through these stories that could aid and apply to anyone. In *Virtue Inverted,* through characters like Dale Beranger, I tried to show that no matter what one has done in his/her past, that person can still have a second chance at living a good and fulfilling life. It also teaches, as Jesus does in the Gospels, that before wrath should come mercy, as Benny and Virtue forgave Dale's horrific deeds and helped him suppress his dark side. These same lessons can be seen in *Amazon Expedient,* but in this current novel, I was mainly exploring the theme of relationship. What do I mean by this? It is my belief that human beings were always meant to live together in caring, compassionate relationships. Regardless of one's race, culture, religious beliefs, etc., we should always treat others with the dignity and respect they deserve. By mistreating and discriminating against people whose ways we may not agree with or understand, we are setting everyone up for disaster. Some people can handle abuse for seemingly infinite periods of time and remain in complete control while others, like Flack, Purp and the Kudgels, reach their breaking point and seek revenge. But the reason for treating people with dignity and respect shouldn't just be because we don't want them to 'freak out,' but because we care for them as human beings and want them to live peaceful lives. Benny and the other characters of this book are able to learn these lessons from each other and their adversaries. Maybe these ideas will help prevent real-life confrontations as well. But then again, it is just fiction.

Writing with Piers Anthony has been a spectacular experience. It has motivated me to get serious with my writing and utilize my skills and imagination. I wrote and worked a lot more for this book than its predecessor: the prologue and epilogue, chapters 1-7 and 11-14. The rest was a combination of my pre-outlined ideas for the story and Mr. Anthony's writing and creative input. His abilities are still far superior to mine, and I knew he would be able to tie this story together in a way I couldn't. I especially appreciate his wife, Cam, for helping us come up with the name for the character Helena the Amazon. I also thank Mr. Anthony and his wife for allowing me to visit and meet them in person, for which I will be eternally grateful. I hope we can continue being friends and collaborators for years to come. Goodbye for now.

About the Authors

Piers Anthony is one of the world's most popular fantasy authors, and a New York Times bestseller twenty-one times over. Anthony is the author of the Xanth series, as well as many other best-selling works. Piers Anthony lives with his wife in Inverness, Florida.

Kenneth Kelly is a 26 year old native of Plant City, Fl. He has been an avid writer his whole life, and has had a number of short works published during grade school and college. He has a Bachelors degree in English Professional Writing from St. Leo University. He is the author of 'Trespassing Through Time.' Outside of writing he is a 3rd degree black belt in Tae Kwon Do.

www.ingramcontent.com/pod-product-compliance
Lightning Source LLC
Chambersburg PA
CBHW022049050726
47591CB00002B/454